THE **HARDY BOYS** ®

UNDERCOVER BROTHERS™

PAPERCUTZ™

THE HARDY BOYS®

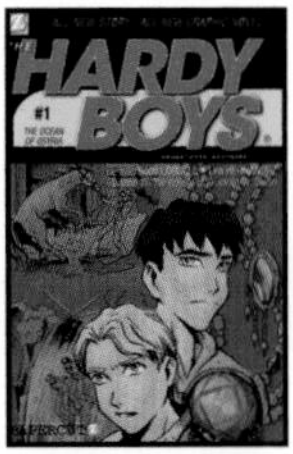
HARDY
BOYS
#1

Graphic Novels
Available from Papercutz
#1 The Ocean of Osyria
#2 Identity Theft
#3 Mad House
#4 Malled
(coming February 2006)
$7.95 each in paperback
$12.95 each in hardcover

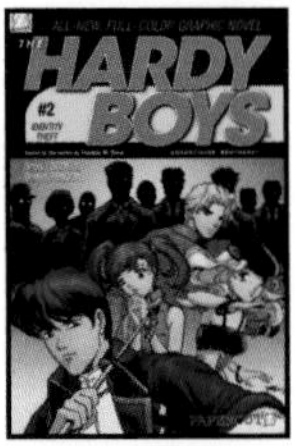
HARDY
BOYS
#2

SPECIAL OFFER!

While supplies last, you may order issues # 2 and # 3 (Sorry, issue # 1 is SOLD OUT!)of the hard-to-find Hardy Boys collector's item comic books, (which were collected in the first Graphic Novel) for $2.95 each!

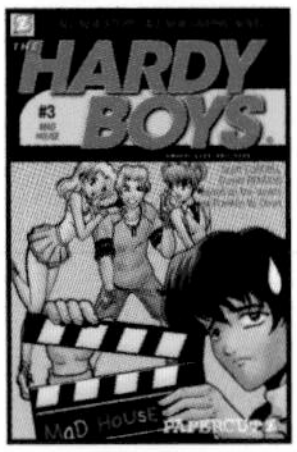
HARDY
BOYS
#3
MaD HOUSE
PAPERCUTZ

Please add $3.00 for postage and handling for the first book, add $1.00 for each additional book.
Send for our catalog:
Papercutz
555 Eighth Avenue, Suite 1202
New York, NY 10018

www.papercutz.com

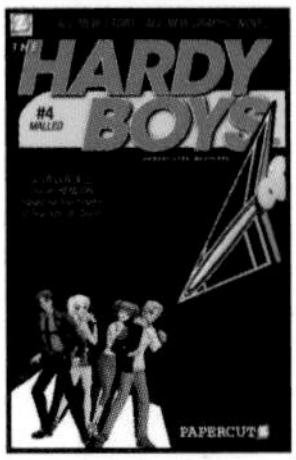
HARDY
BOYS
#4
MALLED
PAPERCUTZ

THE HARDY BOYS

#3

UNDERCOVER BROTHERS™

Mad House

SCOTT LOBDELL • Writer
DANIEL RENDON • Artist
Based on the series by
FRANKLIN W. DIXON

New York

Mad House
SCOTT LOBDELL – Writer
DANIEL RENDON — Artist
BRYAN SENKA – Letterer
LAURIE E. SMITH — Colorist
JIM SALICRUP — Editor-in-Chief

ISBN 10: 1-59707-010-6 paperback edition
ISBN 13: 978-1-59707-010-2 paperback edition
ISBN 10: 1-59707-011-4 hardcover edition
ISBN 13: 978-1-59707-011-9 hardcover edition

10 9 8 7 6 5 4 3 2 1

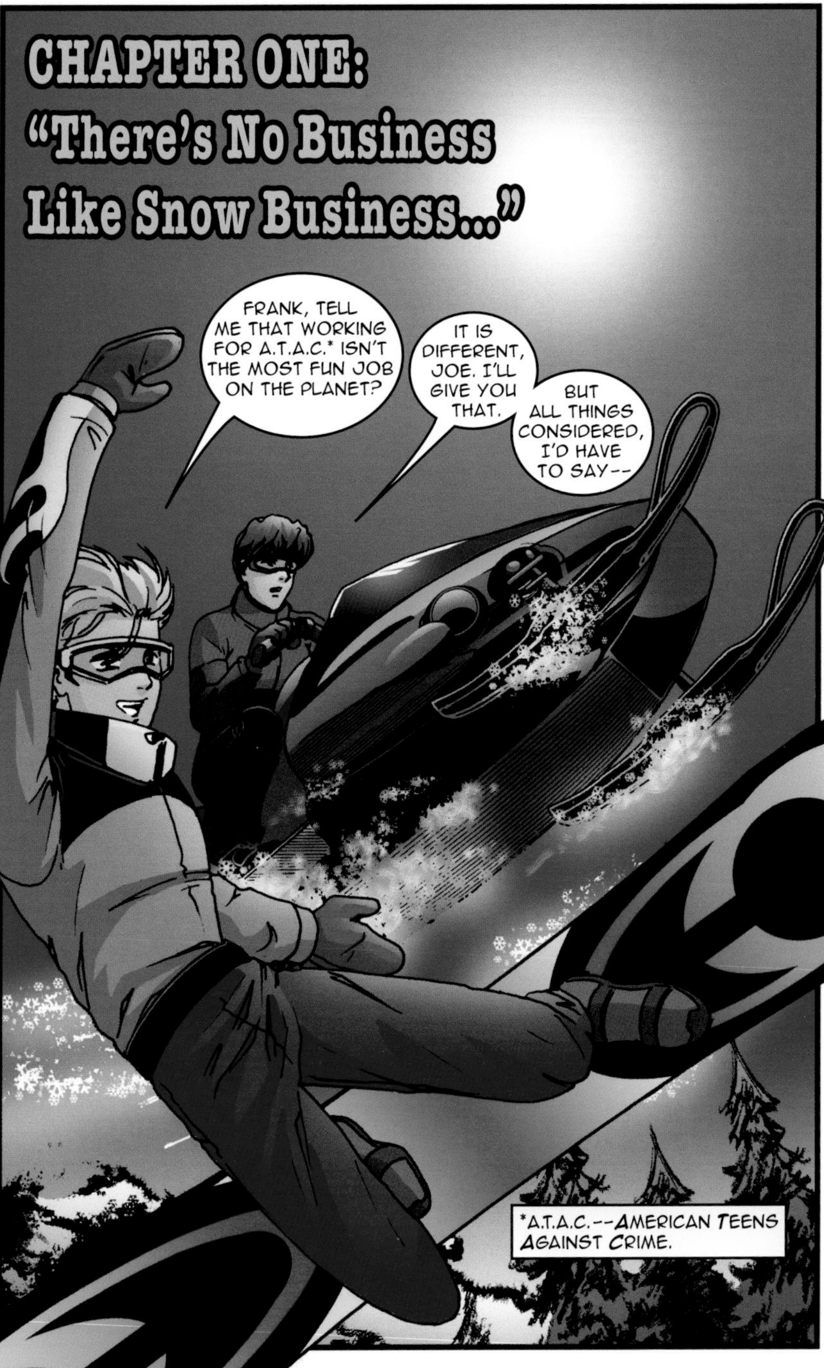
CHAPTER ONE:
"There's No Business Like Snow Business..."
FRANK, TELL ME THAT WORKING FOR A.T.A.C.* ISN'T THE MOST FUN JOB ON THE PLANET?
IT IS DIFFERENT, JOE. I'LL GIVE YOU THAT.
BUT ALL THINGS CONSIDERED, I'D HAVE TO SAY--
*A.T.A.C.--AMERICAN TEENS AGAINST CRIME.

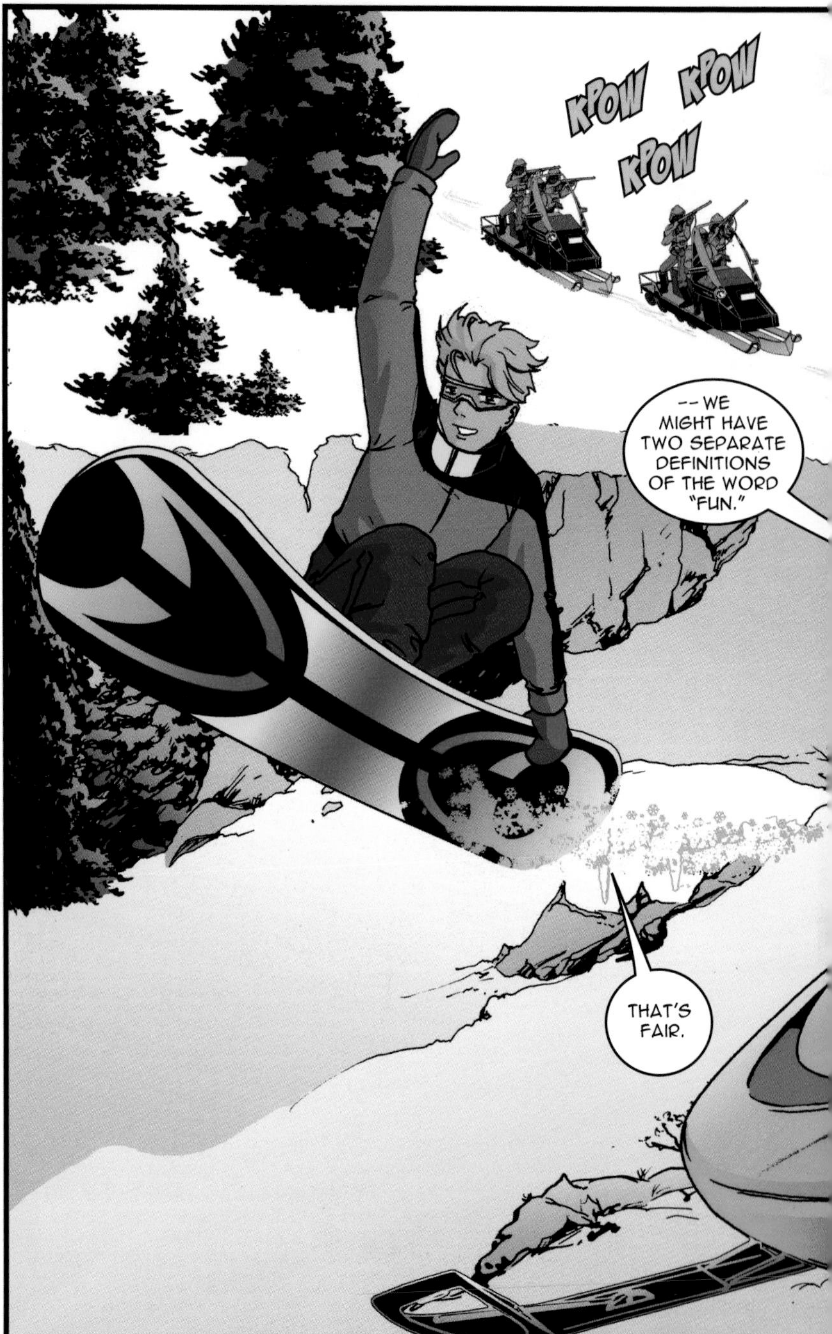
KPOW KPOW
KPOW
--WE MIGHT HAVE TWO SEPARATE DEFINITIONS OF THE WORD "FUN."
THAT'S FAIR.

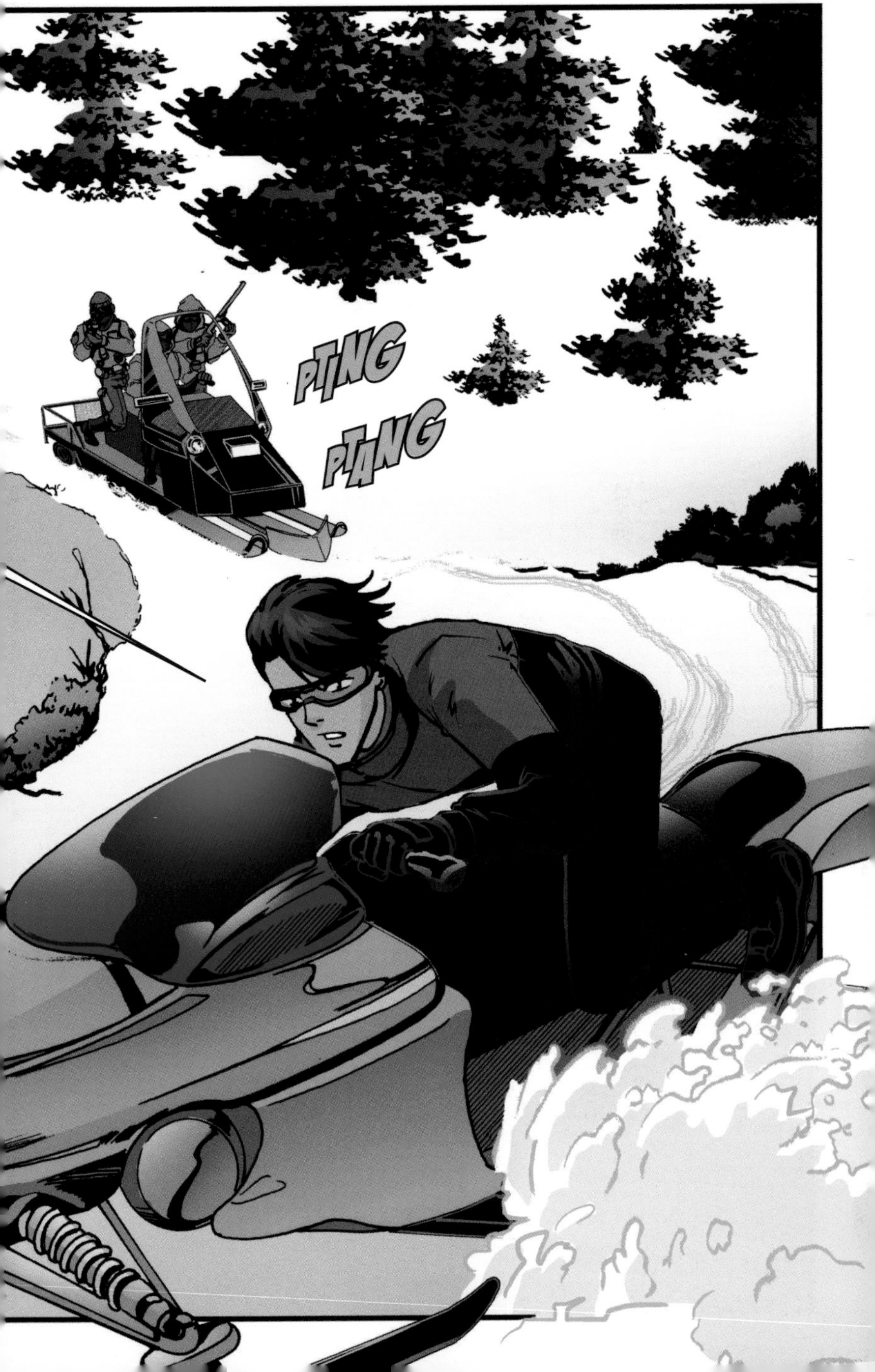
PTING
PTANG

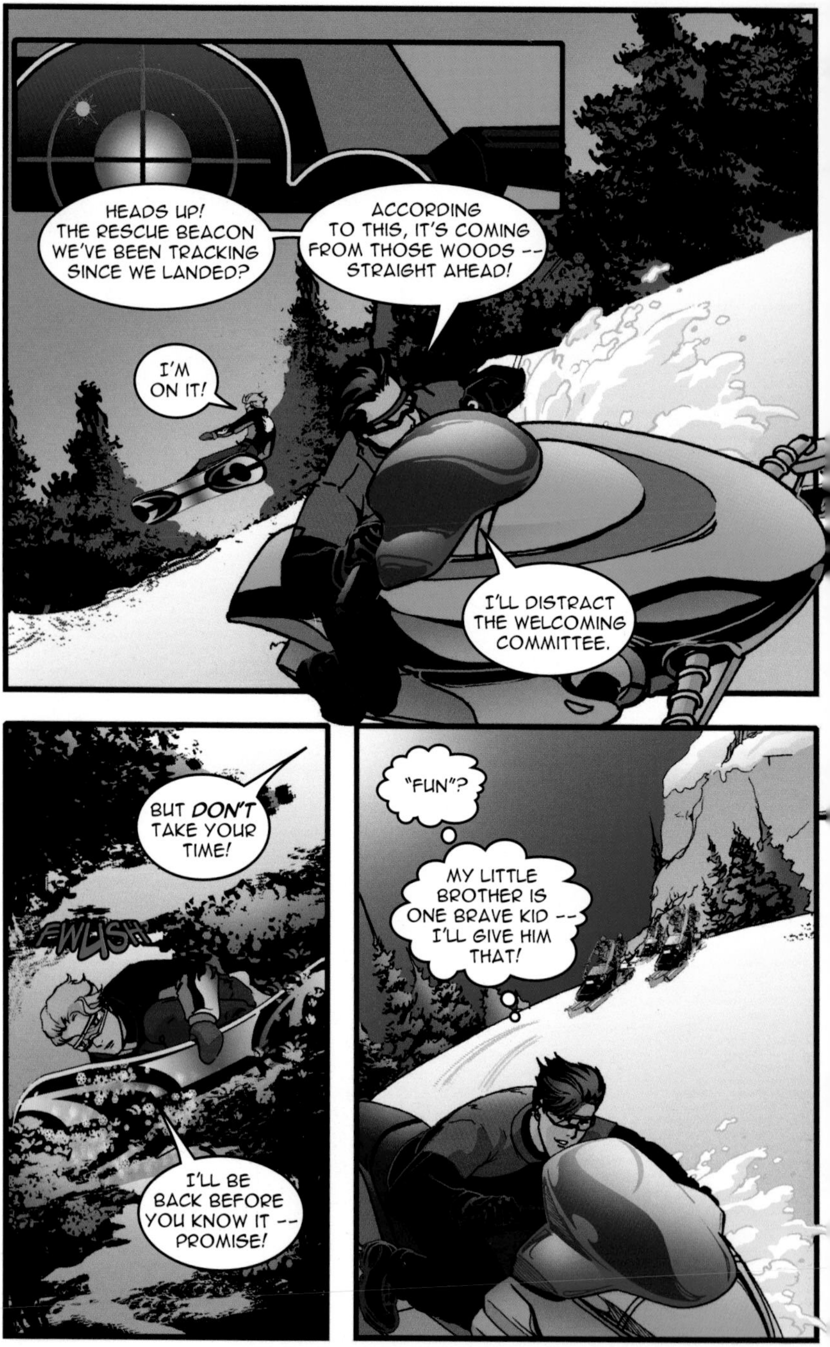
HEADS UP! THE RESCUE BEACON WE'VE BEEN TRACKING SINCE WE LANDED?
ACCORDING TO THIS, IT'S COMING FROM THOSE WOODS -- STRAIGHT AHEAD!
I'M ON IT!
I'LL DISTRACT THE WELCOMING COMMITTEE.
BUT *DON'T* TAKE YOUR TIME!
FWUSH
I'LL BE BACK BEFORE YOU KNOW IT -- PROMISE!
"FUN"?
MY LITTLE BROTHER IS ONE BRAVE KID -- I'LL GIVE HIM THAT!

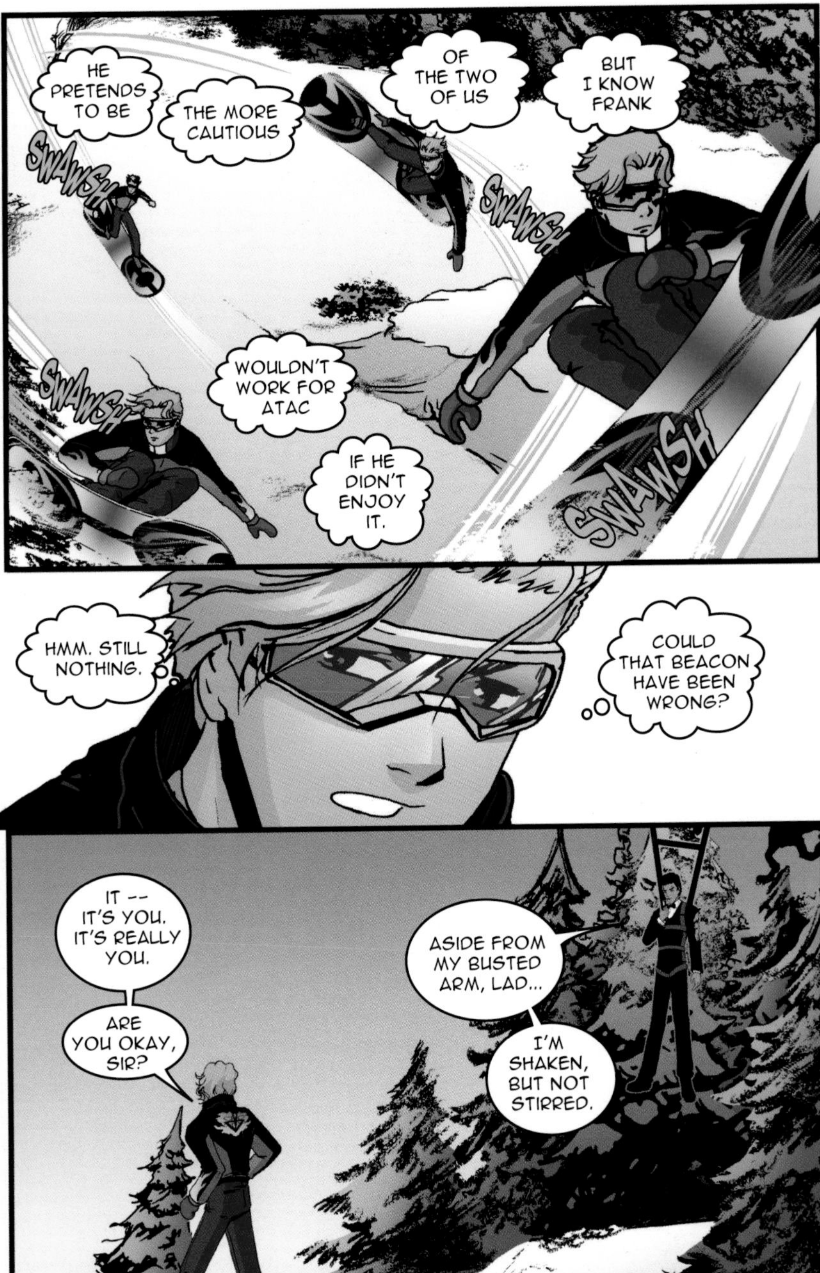
HE PRETENDS TO BE
THE MORE CAUTIOUS
OF THE TWO OF US
BUT I KNOW FRANK
SWAWSH
SWAWSH
SWAWSH
WOULDN'T WORK FOR ATAC
IF HE DIDN'T ENJOY IT.
SWAWSH
HMM. STILL NOTHING.
COULD THAT BEACON HAVE BEEN WRONG?
IT -- IT'S YOU. IT'S REALLY YOU.
ARE YOU OKAY, SIR?
ASIDE FROM MY BUSTED ARM, LAD...
I'M SHAKEN, BUT NOT STIRRED.

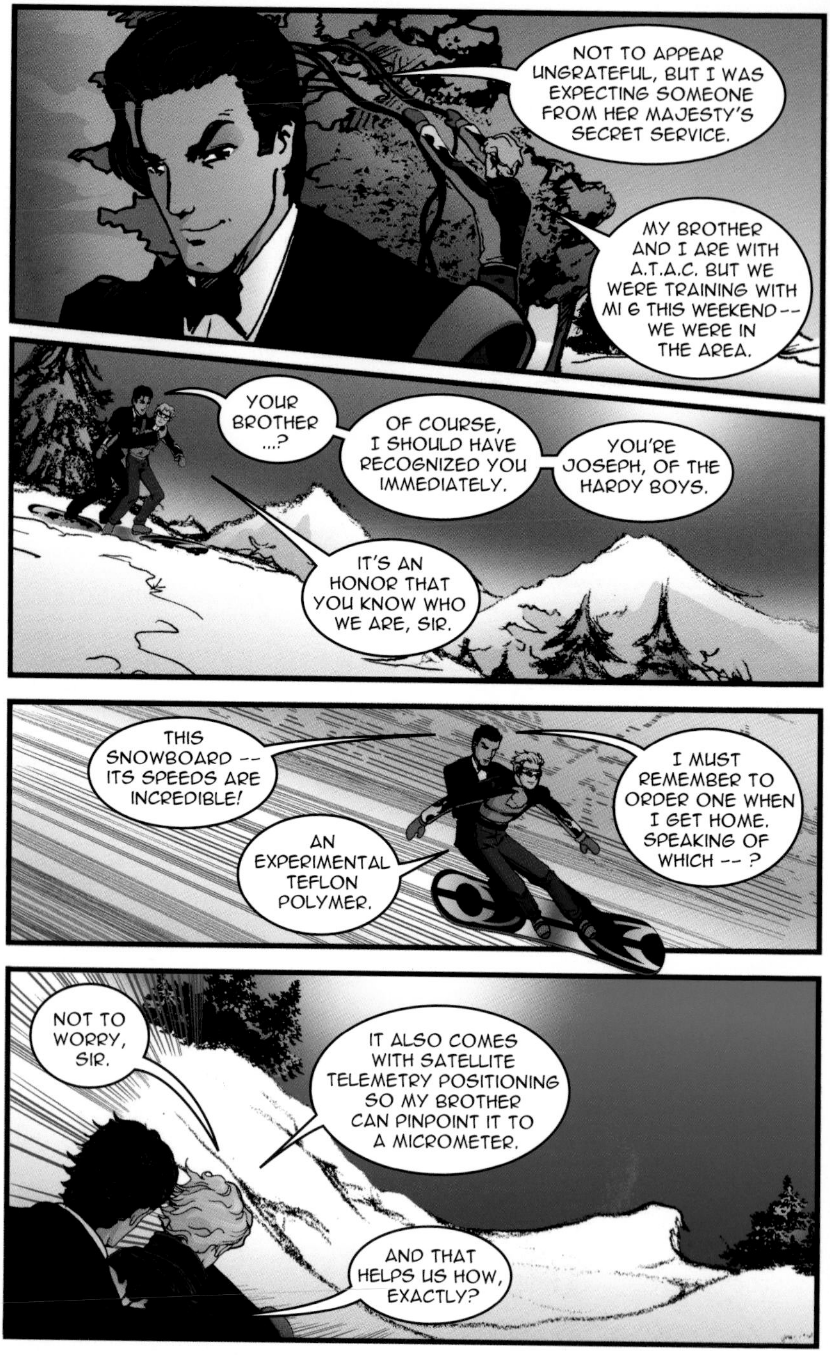
NOT TO APPEAR UNGRATEFUL, BUT I WAS EXPECTING SOMEONE FROM HER MAJESTY'S SECRET SERVICE.
MY BROTHER AND I ARE WITH A.T.A.C. BUT WE WERE TRAINING WITH MI 6 THIS WEEKEND-- WE WERE IN THE AREA.
YOUR BROTHER ...?
OF COURSE, I SHOULD HAVE RECOGNIZED YOU IMMEDIATELY.
YOU'RE JOSEPH, OF THE HARDY BOYS.
IT'S AN HONOR THAT YOU KNOW WHO WE ARE, SIR.
THIS SNOWBOARD -- ITS SPEEDS ARE INCREDIBLE!
AN EXPERIMENTAL TEFLON POLYMER.
I MUST REMEMBER TO ORDER ONE WHEN I GET HOME. SPEAKING OF WHICH -- ?
NOT TO WORRY, SIR.
IT ALSO COMES WITH SATELLITE TELEMETRY POSITIONING SO MY BROTHER CAN PINPOINT IT TO A MICROMETER.
AND THAT HELPS US HOW, EXACTLY?

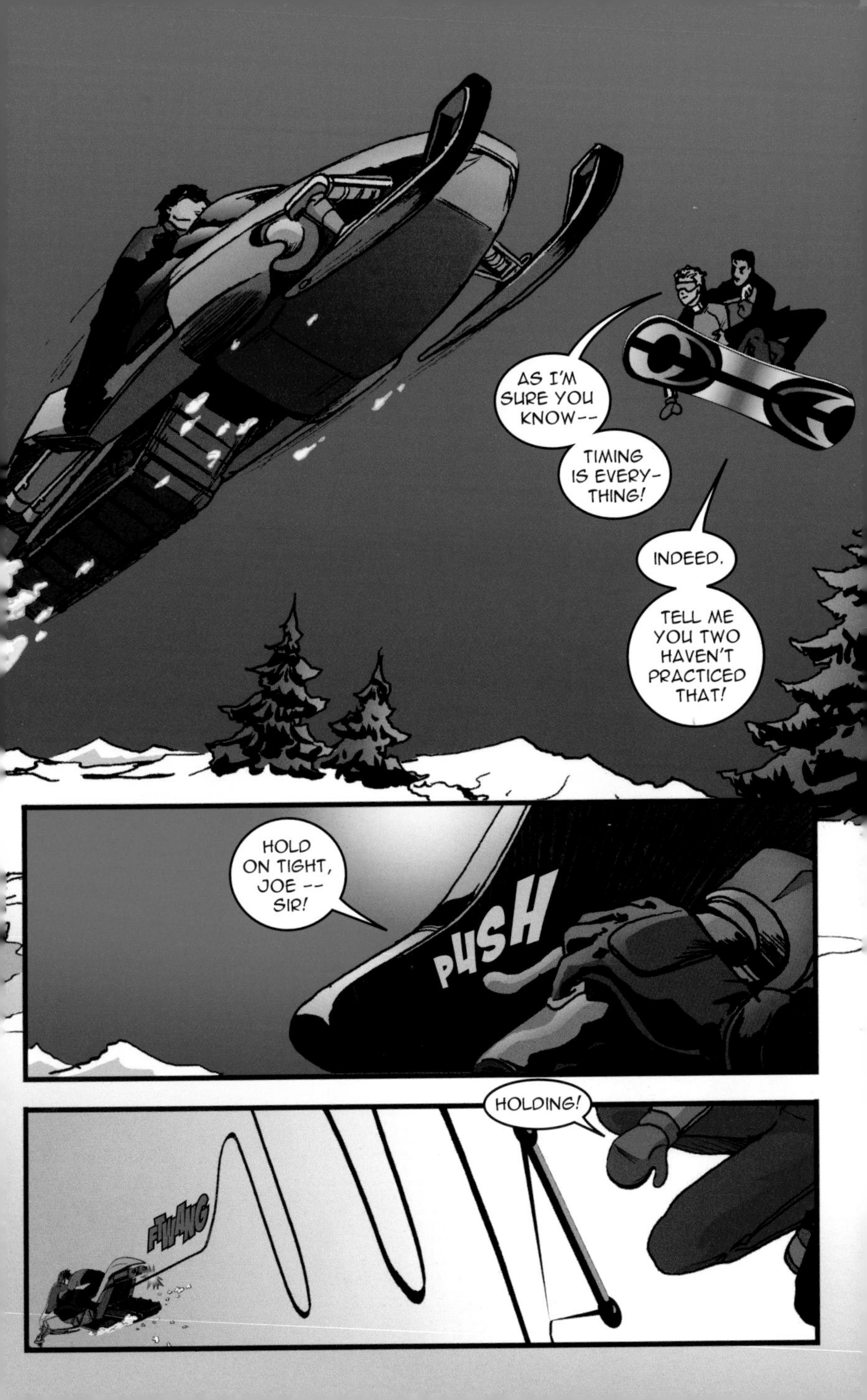
AS I'M SURE YOU KNOW--
TIMING IS EVERY-THING!
INDEED.
TELL ME YOU TWO HAVEN'T PRACTICED THAT!
HOLD ON TIGHT, JOE -- SIR!
PUSH
HOLDING!
FTWANG

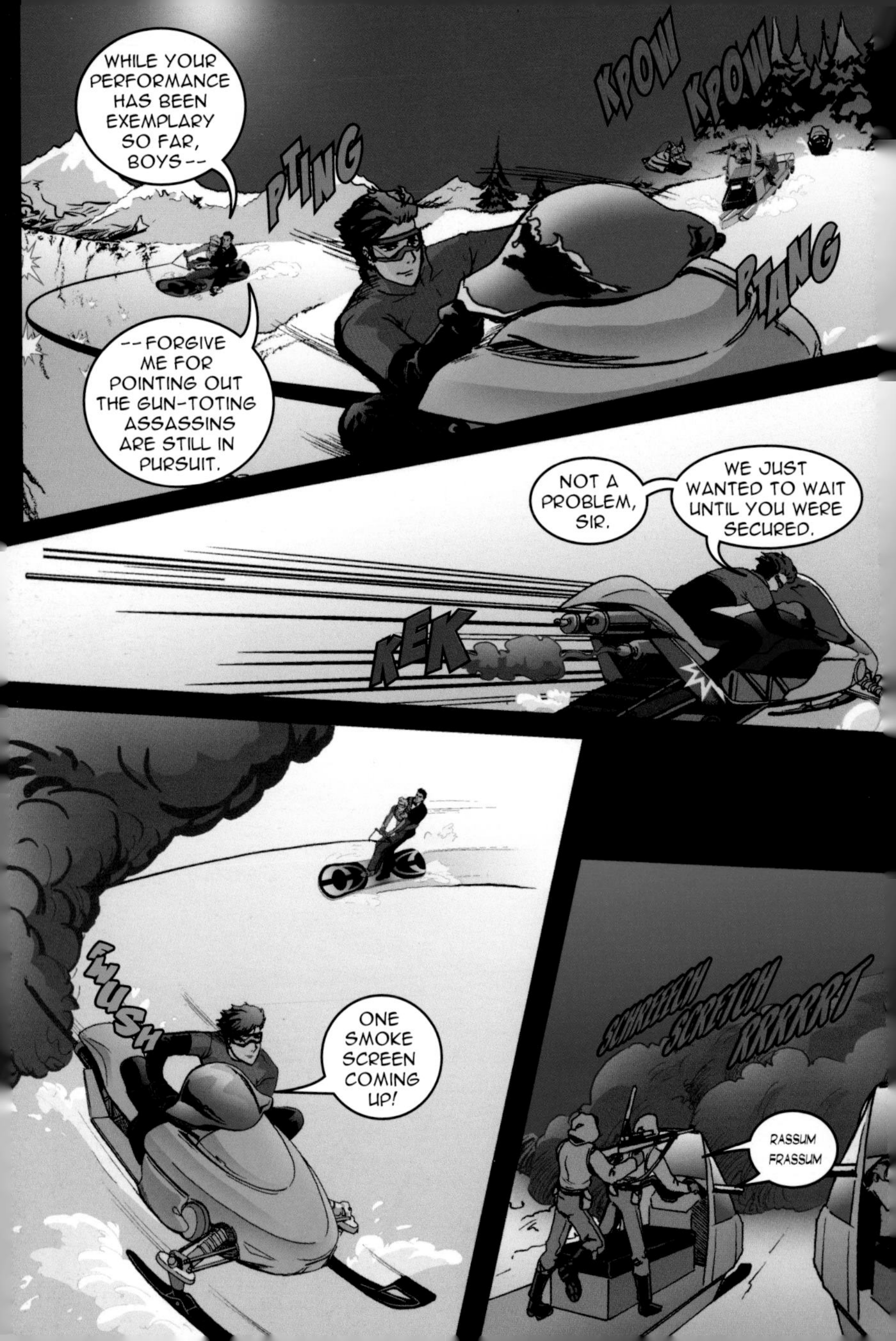
WHILE YOUR PERFORMANCE HAS BEEN EXEMPLARY SO FAR, BOYS--
KPOW
KPOW
PTING
PTANG
--FORGIVE ME FOR POINTING OUT THE GUN-TOTING ASSASSINS ARE STILL IN PURSUIT.
NOT A PROBLEM, SIR.
WE JUST WANTED TO WAIT UNTIL YOU WERE SECURED.
KEK
FWUSH
ONE SMOKE SCREEN COMING UP!
SCHREEERCH
SCREETCH
KRRRRRT
RASSUM FRASSUM

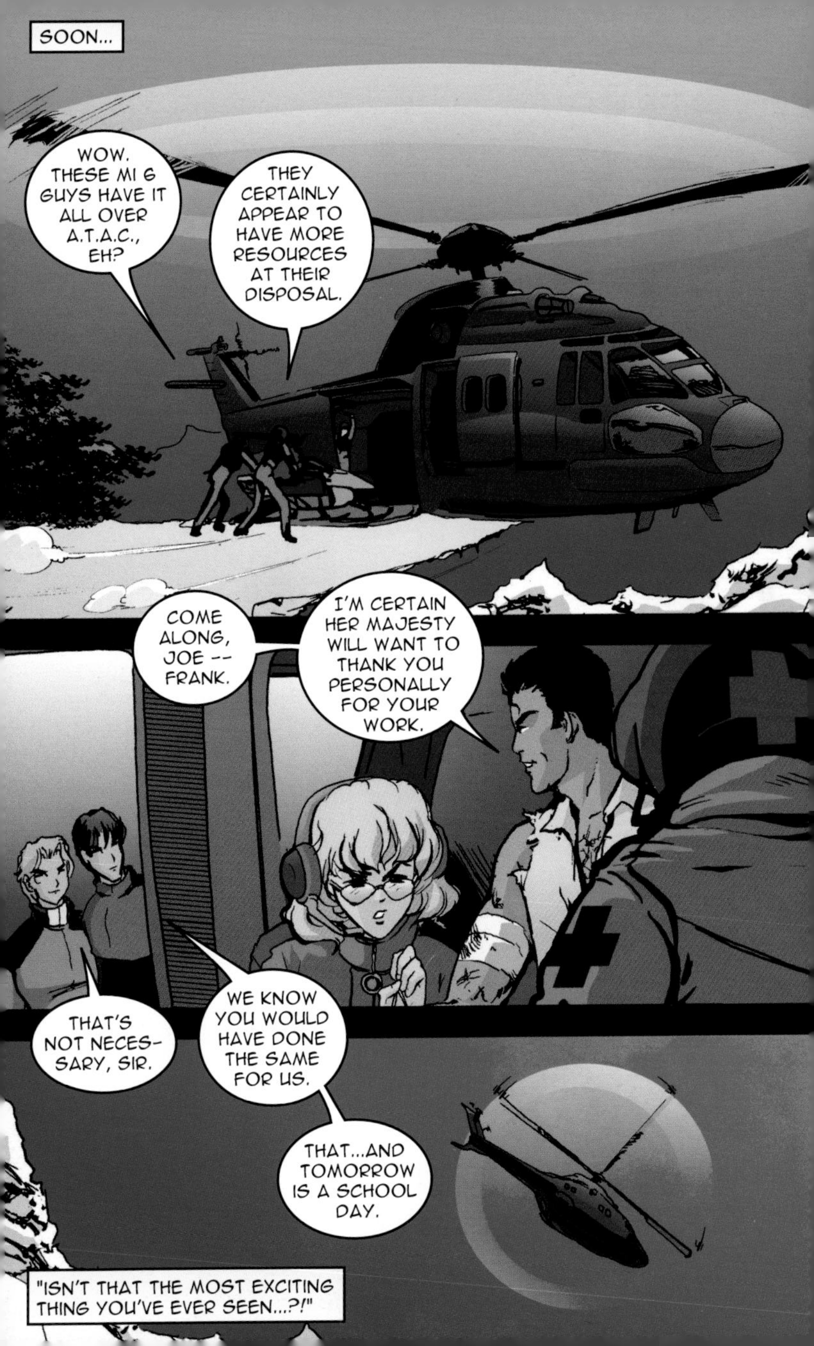
SOON...
WOW. THESE MI 6 GUYS HAVE IT ALL OVER A.T.A.C., EH?
THEY CERTAINLY APPEAR TO HAVE MORE RESOURCES AT THEIR DISPOSAL.
COME ALONG, JOE -- FRANK.
I'M CERTAIN HER MAJESTY WILL WANT TO THANK YOU PERSONALLY FOR YOUR WORK.
THAT'S NOT NECES-SARY, SIR.
WE KNOW YOU WOULD HAVE DONE THE SAME FOR US.
THAT...AND TOMORROW IS A SCHOOL DAY.
"ISN'T THAT THE MOST EXCITING THING YOU'VE EVER SEEN...?!"

CHAPTER TWO: "Thanks, But No..."

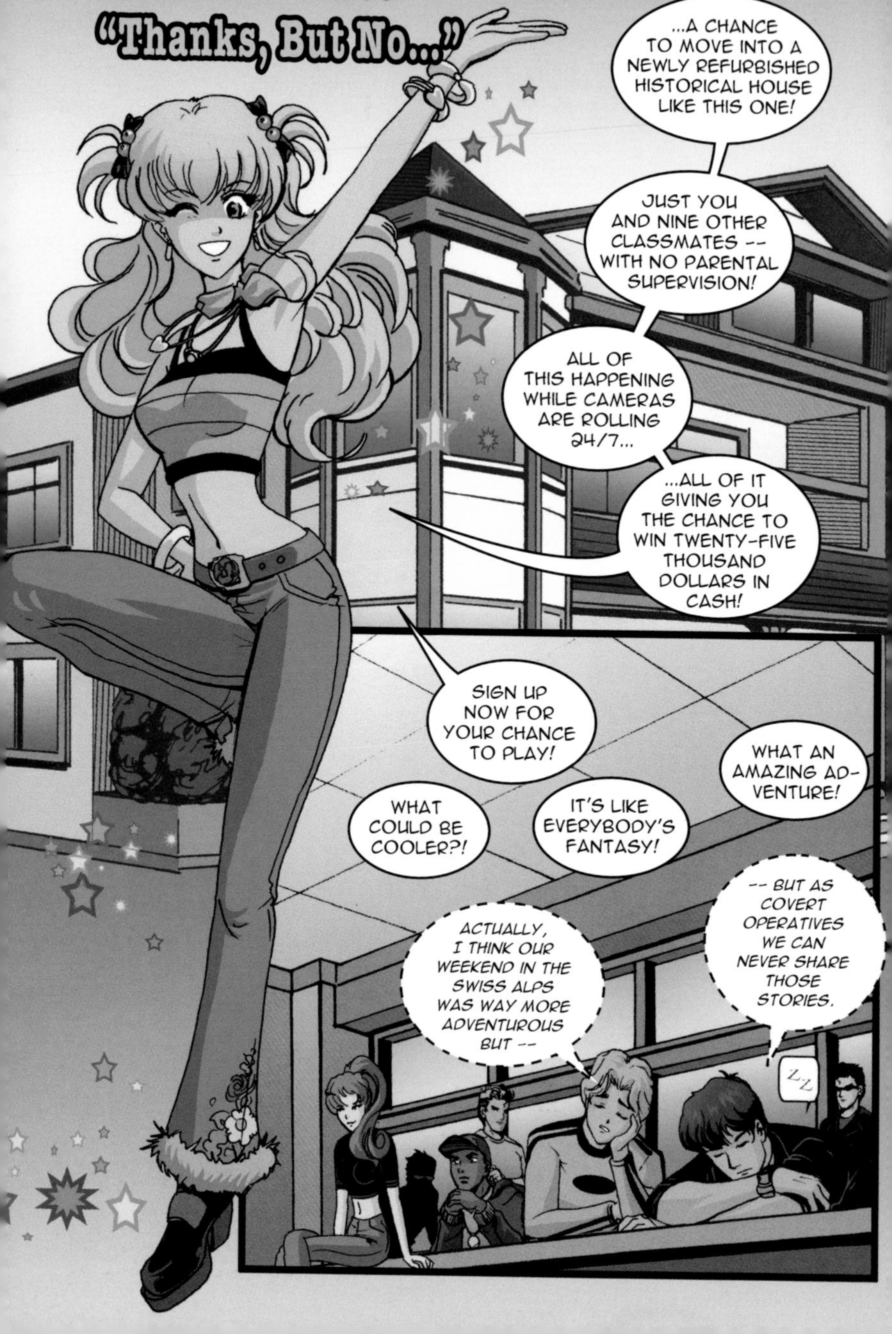

...A CHANCE TO MOVE INTO A NEWLY REFURBISHED HISTORICAL HOUSE LIKE THIS ONE!
JUST YOU AND NINE OTHER CLASSMATES -- WITH NO PARENTAL SUPERVISION!
ALL OF THIS HAPPENING WHILE CAMERAS ARE ROLLING 24/7...
...ALL OF IT GIVING YOU THE CHANCE TO WIN TWENTY-FIVE THOUSAND DOLLARS IN CASH!
SIGN UP NOW FOR YOUR CHANCE TO PLAY!
WHAT AN AMAZING AD-VENTURE!
IT'S LIKE EVERYBODY'S FANTASY!
WHAT COULD BE COOLER?!
ACTUALLY, I THINK OUR WEEKEND IN THE SWISS ALPS WAS WAY MORE ADVENTUROUS BUT --
-- BUT AS COVERT OPERATIVES WE CAN NEVER SHARE THOSE STORIES.
Z Z

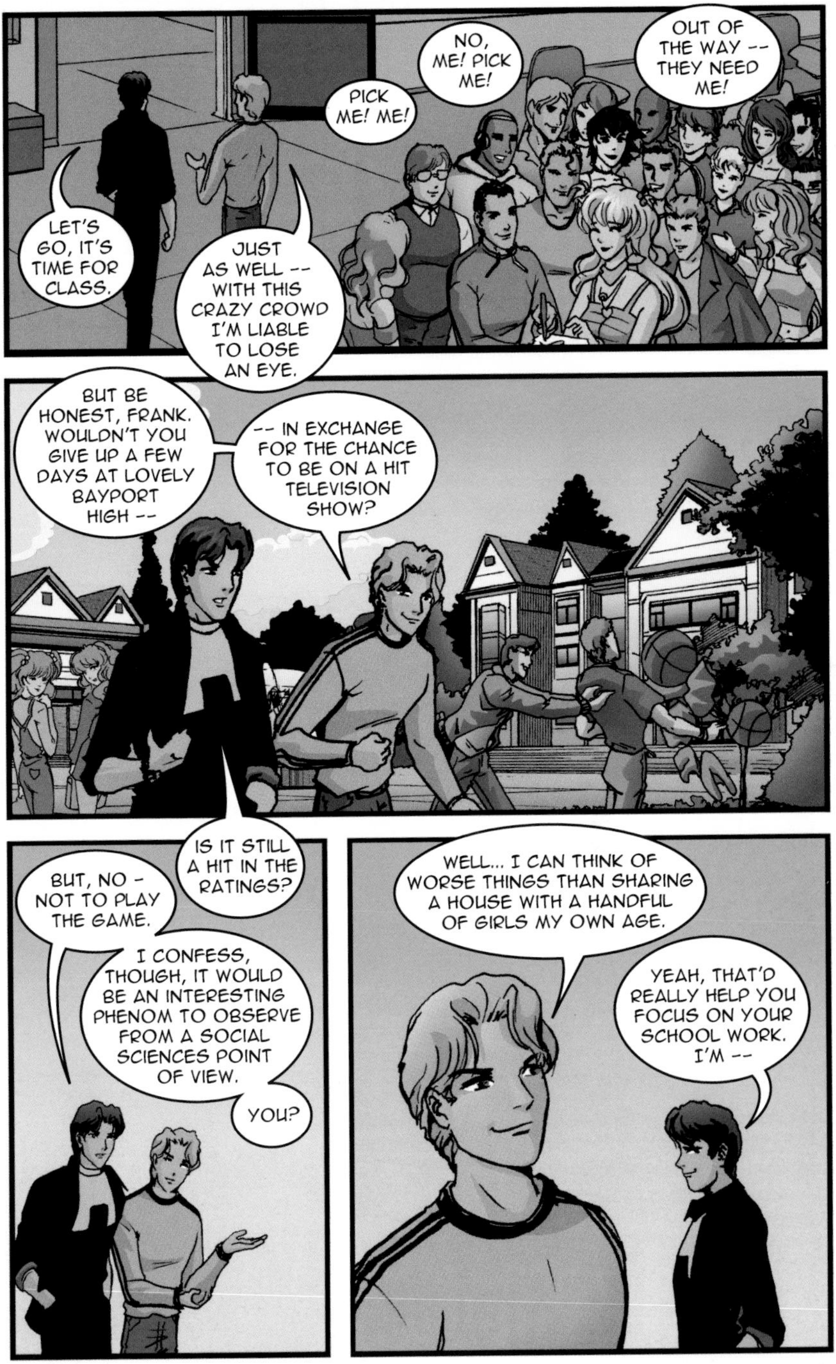

PICK ME! ME!
NO, ME! PICK ME!
OUT OF THE WAY -- THEY NEED ME!
LET'S GO, IT'S TIME FOR CLASS.
JUST AS WELL -- WITH THIS CRAZY CROWD I'M LIABLE TO LOSE AN EYE.
BUT BE HONEST, FRANK. WOULDN'T YOU GIVE UP A FEW DAYS AT LOVELY BAYPORT HIGH --
-- IN EXCHANGE FOR THE CHANCE TO BE ON A HIT TELEVISION SHOW?
IS IT STILL A HIT IN THE RATINGS?
BUT, NO - NOT TO PLAY THE GAME.
I CONFESS, THOUGH, IT WOULD BE AN INTERESTING PHENOM TO OBSERVE FROM A SOCIAL SCIENCES POINT OF VIEW.
YOU?
WELL... I CAN THINK OF WORSE THINGS THAN SHARING A HOUSE WITH A HANDFUL OF GIRLS MY OWN AGE.
YEAH, THAT'D REALLY HELP YOU FOCUS ON YOUR SCHOOL WORK. I'M --

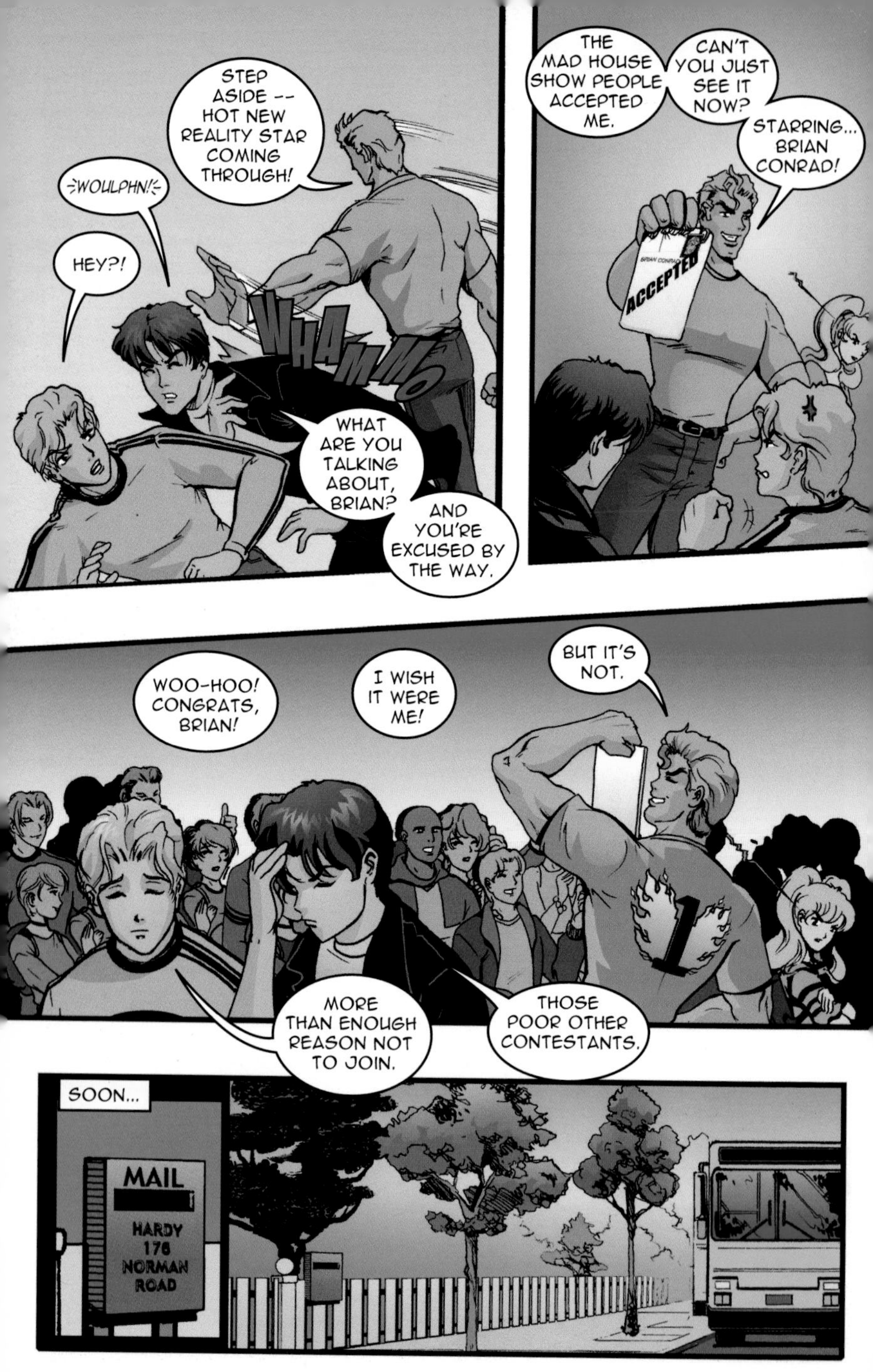
STEP ASIDE -- HOT NEW REALITY STAR COMING THROUGH!
WOULPHN!
HEY?!
WHAMMO
WHAT ARE YOU TALKING ABOUT, BRIAN?
AND YOU'RE EXCUSED BY THE WAY.
THE MAD HOUSE SHOW PEOPLE ACCEPTED ME.
CAN'T YOU JUST SEE IT NOW?
STARRING... BRIAN CONRAD!
ACCEPTED
WOO-HOO! CONGRATS, BRIAN!
I WISH IT WERE ME!
BUT IT'S NOT.
THOSE POOR OTHER CONTESTANTS.
MORE THAN ENOUGH REASON NOT TO JOIN.
SOON...
MAIL
HARDY
176
NORMAN
ROAD

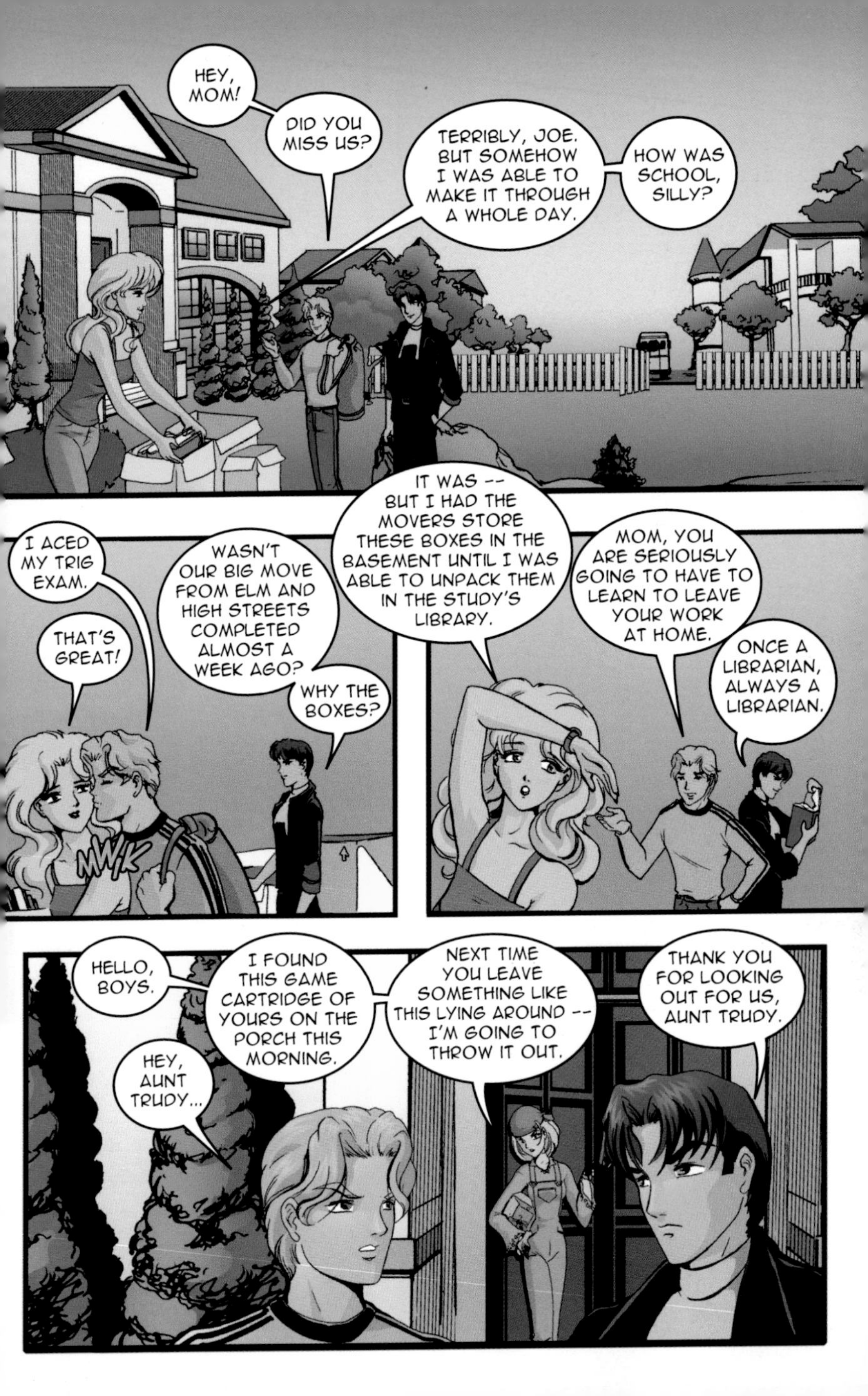

HEY, MOM!
DID YOU MISS US?
TERRIBLY, JOE. BUT SOMEHOW I WAS ABLE TO MAKE IT THROUGH A WHOLE DAY.
HOW WAS SCHOOL, SILLY?
I ACED MY TRIG EXAM.
THAT'S GREAT!
MWAK
WASN'T OUR BIG MOVE FROM ELM AND HIGH STREETS COMPLETED ALMOST A WEEK AGO?
WHY THE BOXES?
IT WAS -- BUT I HAD THE MOVERS STORE THESE BOXES IN THE BASEMENT UNTIL I WAS ABLE TO UNPACK THEM IN THE STUDY'S LIBRARY.
MOM, YOU ARE SERIOUSLY GOING TO HAVE TO LEARN TO LEAVE YOUR WORK AT HOME.
ONCE A LIBRARIAN, ALWAYS A LIBRARIAN.
HELLO, BOYS.
HEY, AUNT TRUDY...
I FOUND THIS GAME CARTRIDGE OF YOURS ON THE PORCH THIS MORNING.
NEXT TIME YOU LEAVE SOMETHING LIKE THIS LYING AROUND -- I'M GOING TO THROW IT OUT.
THANK YOU FOR LOOKING OUT FOR US, AUNT TRUDY.

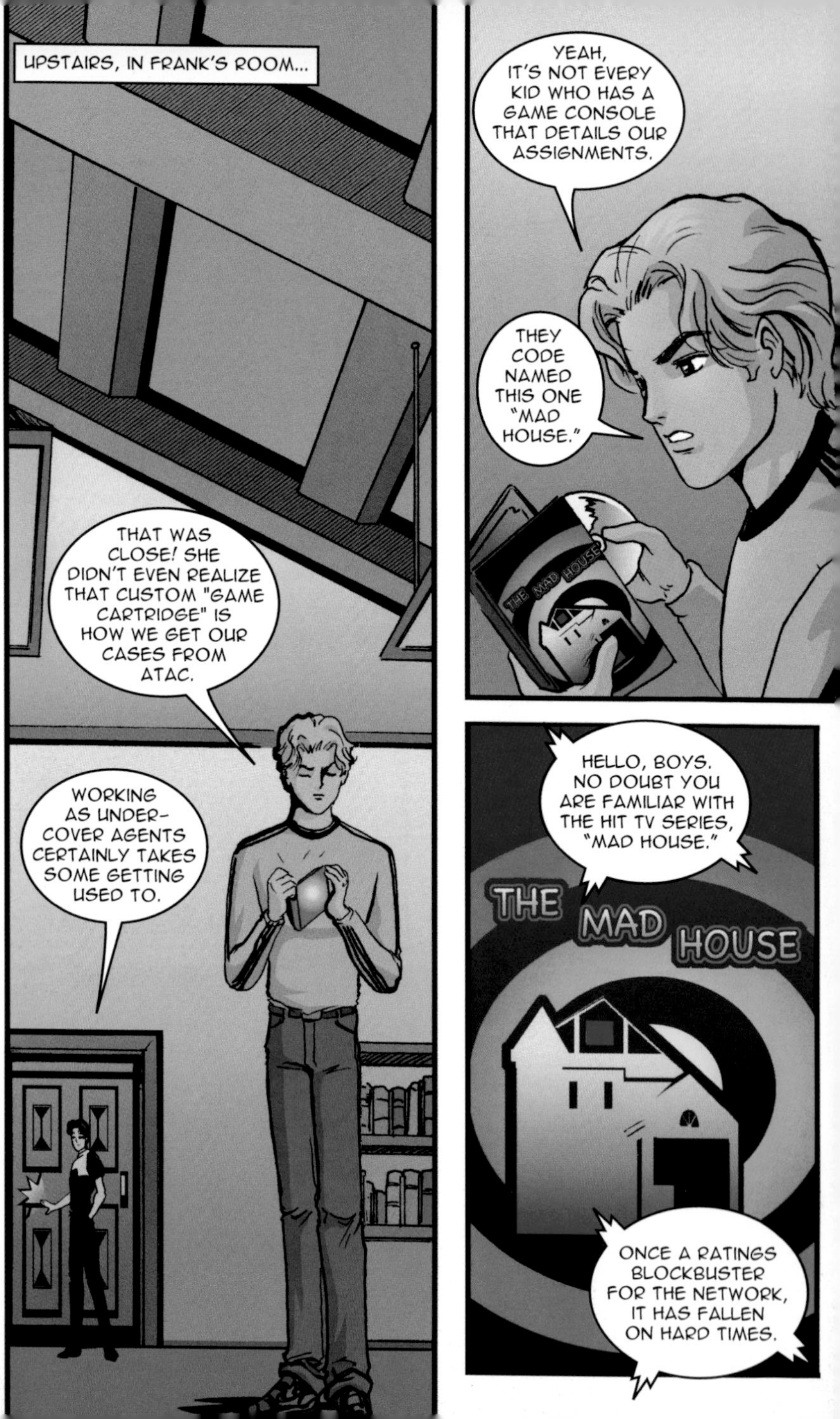
UPSTAIRS, IN FRANK'S ROOM...
THAT WAS CLOSE! SHE DIDN'T EVEN REALIZE THAT CUSTOM "GAME CARTRIDGE" IS HOW WE GET OUR CASES FROM ATAC.
WORKING AS UNDER-COVER AGENTS CERTAINLY TAKES SOME GETTING USED TO.
YEAH, IT'S NOT EVERY KID WHO HAS A GAME CONSOLE THAT DETAILS OUR ASSIGNMENTS.
THEY CODE NAMED THIS ONE "MAD HOUSE."
THE MAD HOUSE
HELLO, BOYS. NO DOUBT YOU ARE FAMILIAR WITH THE HIT TV SERIES, "MAD HOUSE."
THE MAD HOUSE
ONCE A RATINGS BLOCKBUSTER FOR THE NETWORK, IT HAS FALLEN ON HARD TIMES.

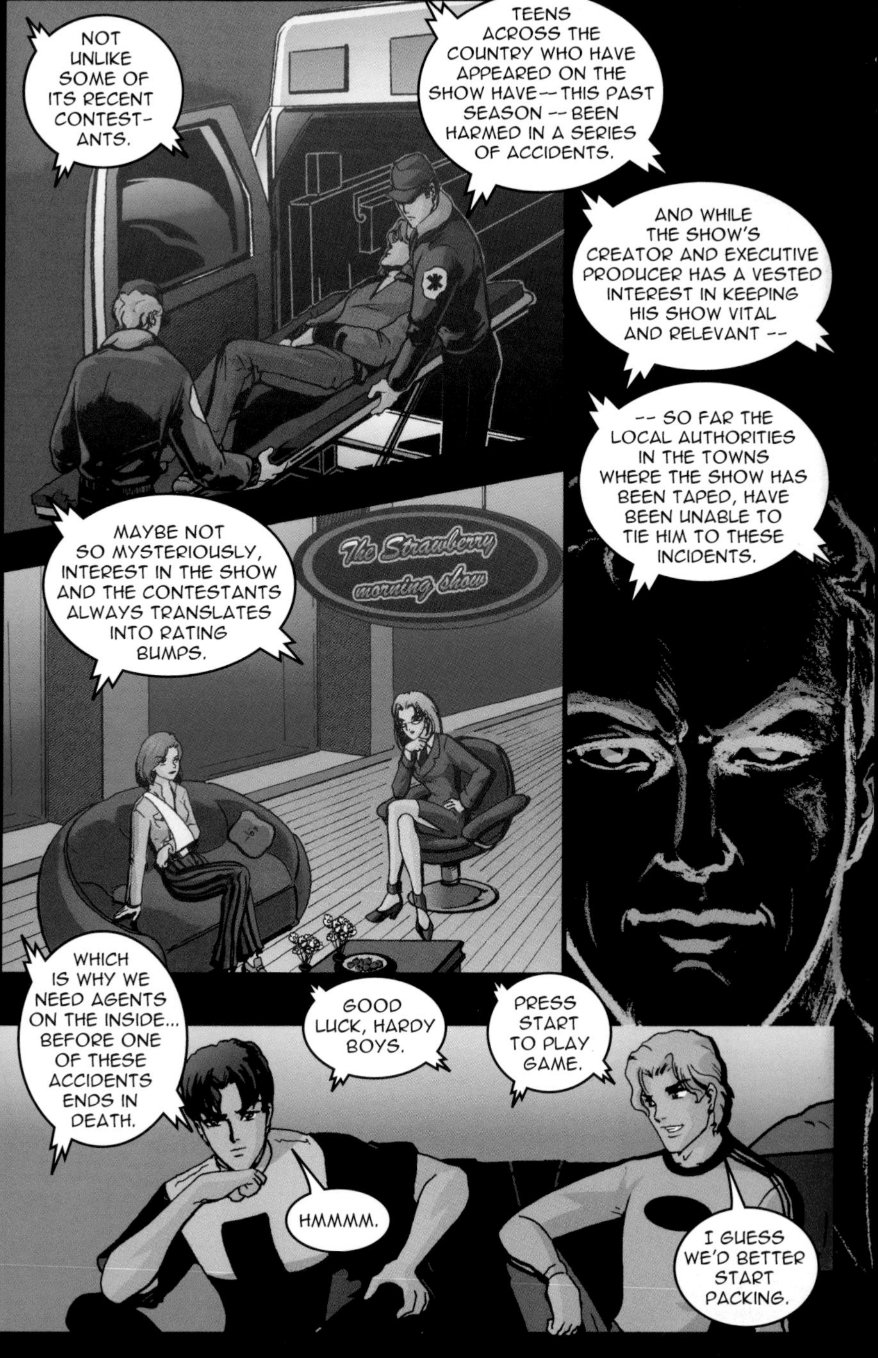
NOT UNLIKE SOME OF ITS RECENT CONTEST-ANTS.
TEENS ACROSS THE COUNTRY WHO HAVE APPEARED ON THE SHOW HAVE-- THIS PAST SEASON -- BEEN HARMED IN A SERIES OF ACCIDENTS.
AND WHILE THE SHOW'S CREATOR AND EXECUTIVE PRODUCER HAS A VESTED INTEREST IN KEEPING HIS SHOW VITAL AND RELEVANT --
-- SO FAR THE LOCAL AUTHORITIES IN THE TOWNS WHERE THE SHOW HAS BEEN TAPED, HAVE BEEN UNABLE TO TIE HIM TO THESE INCIDENTS.
MAYBE NOT SO MYSTERIOUSLY, INTEREST IN THE SHOW AND THE CONTESTANTS ALWAYS TRANSLATES INTO RATING BUMPS.
The Strawberry morning show
WHICH IS WHY WE NEED AGENTS ON THE INSIDE... BEFORE ONE OF THESE ACCIDENTS ENDS IN DEATH.
GOOD LUCK, HARDY BOYS.
PRESS START TO PLAY GAME.
HMMMM.
I GUESS WE'D BETTER START PACKING.

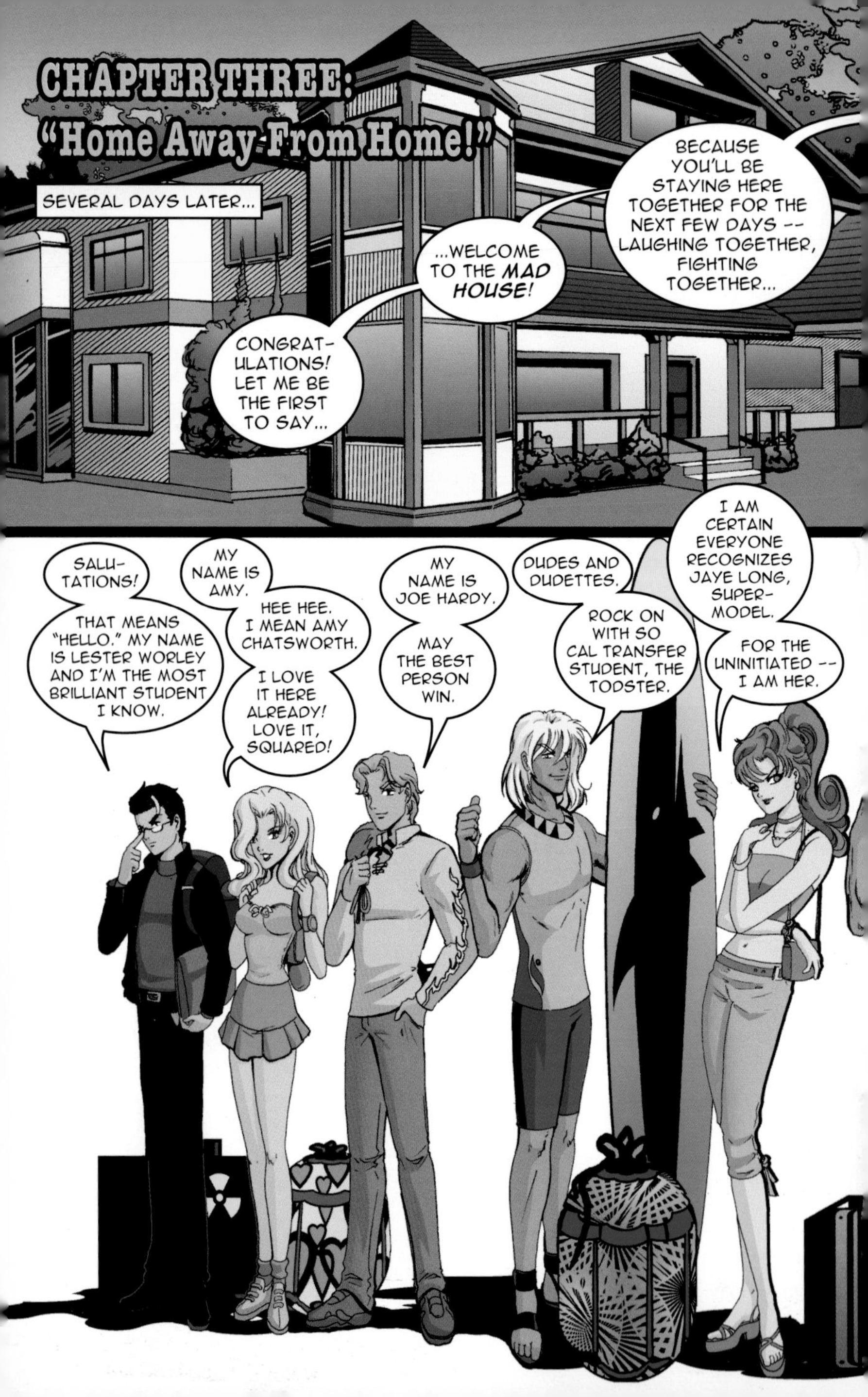
CHAPTER THREE:
"Home Away From Home!"
SEVERAL DAYS LATER...
CONGRATULATIONS! LET ME BE THE FIRST TO SAY...
...WELCOME TO THE *MAD HOUSE*!
BECAUSE YOU'LL BE STAYING HERE TOGETHER FOR THE NEXT FEW DAYS -- LAUGHING TOGETHER, FIGHTING TOGETHER...
SALUTATIONS!
THAT MEANS "HELLO." MY NAME IS LESTER WORLEY AND I'M THE MOST BRILLIANT STUDENT I KNOW.
MY NAME IS AMY.
HEE HEE. I MEAN AMY CHATSWORTH.
I LOVE IT HERE ALREADY! LOVE IT, SQUARED!
MY NAME IS JOE HARDY.
MAY THE BEST PERSON WIN.
DUDES AND DUDETTES.
ROCK ON WITH SO CAL TRANSFER STUDENT, THE TODSTER.
I AM CERTAIN EVERYONE RECOGNIZES JAYE LONG, SUPER-MODEL.
FOR THE UNINITIATED -- I AM HER.

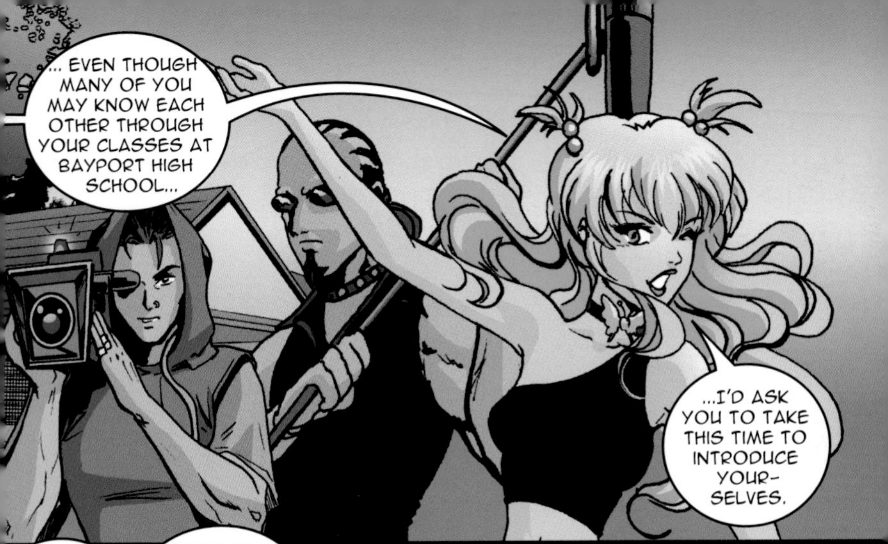
... EVEN THOUGH MANY OF YOU MAY KNOW EACH OTHER THROUGH YOUR CLASSES AT BAYPORT HIGH SCHOOL...
...I'D ASK YOU TO TAKE THIS TIME TO INTRODUCE YOUR-SELVES.

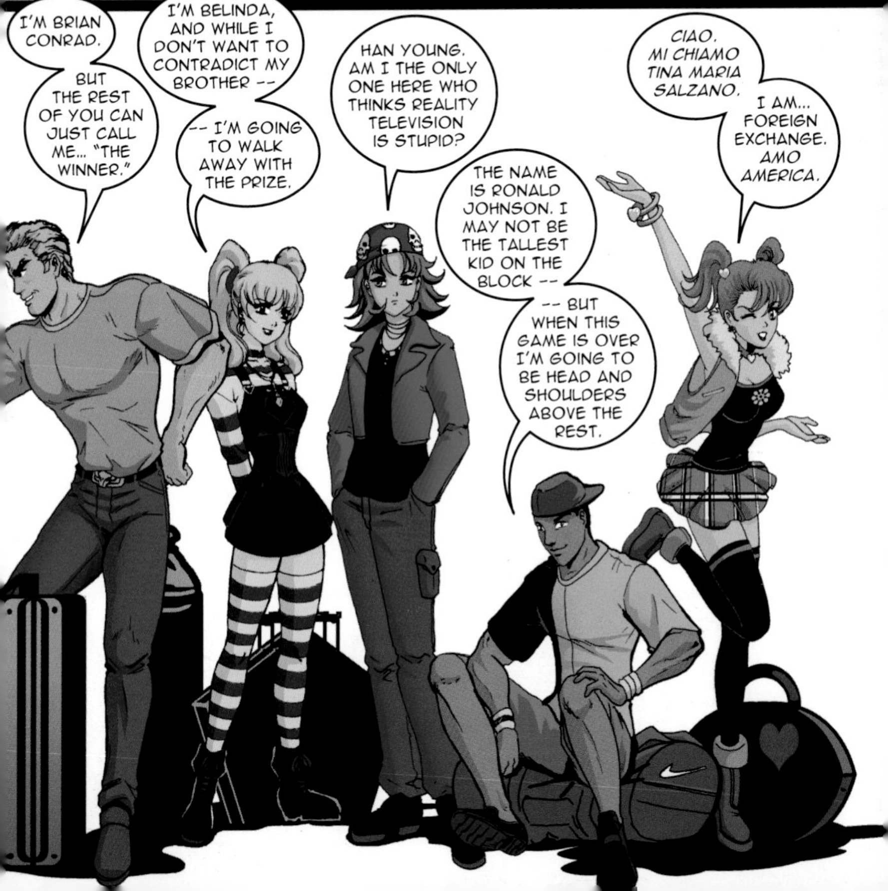
I'M BRIAN CONRAD.
BUT THE REST OF YOU CAN JUST CALL ME... "THE WINNER."
I'M BELINDA, AND WHILE I DON'T WANT TO CONTRADICT MY BROTHER --
-- I'M GOING TO WALK AWAY WITH THE PRIZE.
HAN YOUNG. AM I THE ONLY ONE HERE WHO THINKS REALITY TELEVISION IS STUPID?
THE NAME IS RONALD JOHNSON. I MAY NOT BE THE TALLEST KID ON THE BLOCK --
-- BUT WHEN THIS GAME IS OVER I'M GOING TO BE HEAD AND SHOULDERS ABOVE THE REST.
CIAO. MI CHIAMO TINA MARIA SALZANO.
I AM... FOREIGN EXCHANGE. AMO AMERICA.

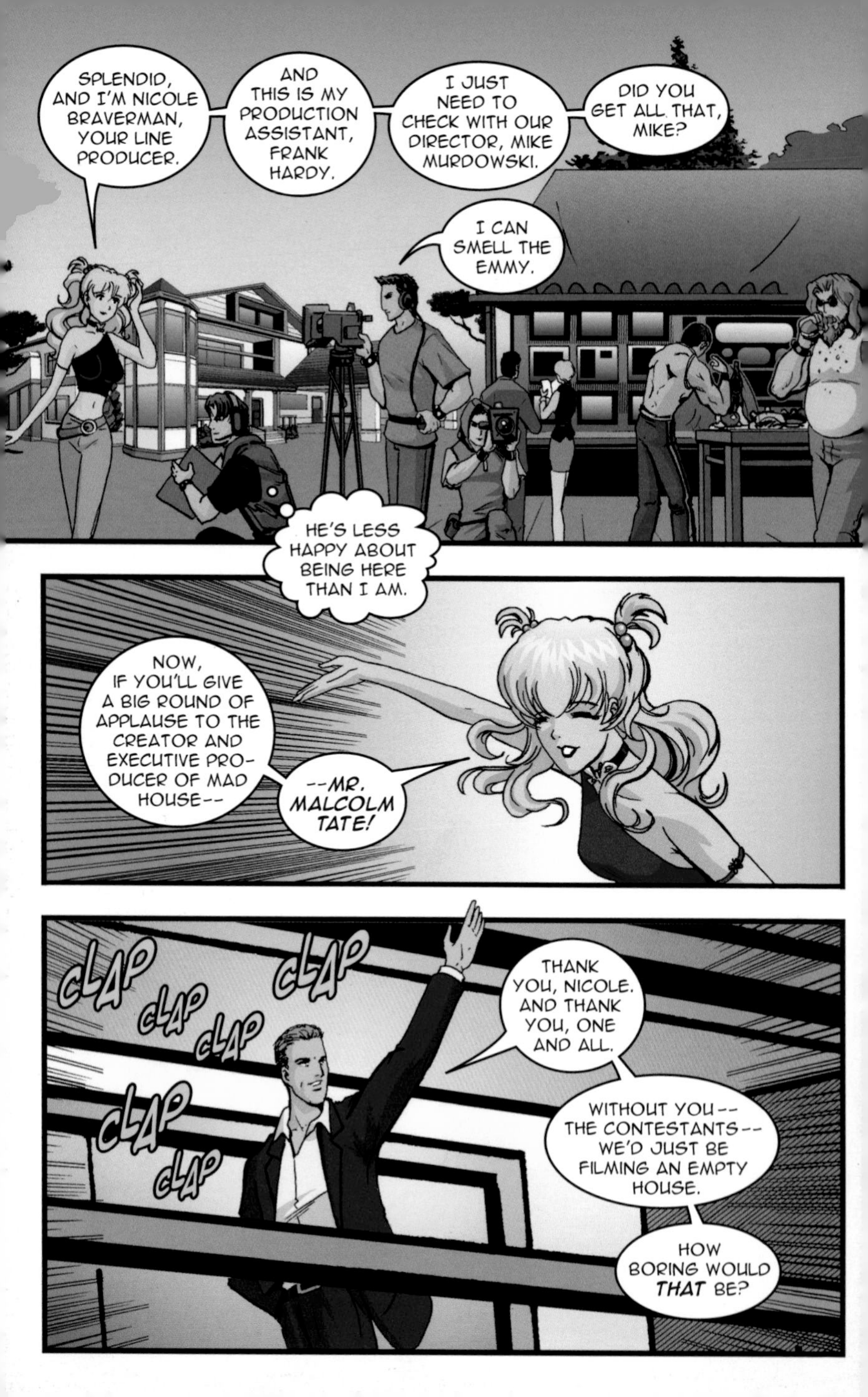
SPLENDID, AND I'M NICOLE BRAVERMAN, YOUR LINE PRODUCER.
AND THIS IS MY PRODUCTION ASSISTANT, FRANK HARDY.
I JUST NEED TO CHECK WITH OUR DIRECTOR, MIKE MURDOWSKI.
DID YOU GET ALL THAT, MIKE?
I CAN SMELL THE EMMY.
HE'S LESS HAPPY ABOUT BEING HERE THAN I AM.
NOW, IF YOU'LL GIVE A BIG ROUND OF APPLAUSE TO THE CREATOR AND EXECUTIVE PRO-DUCER OF MAD HOUSE--
--MR. MALCOLM TATE!
CLAP
CLAP
CLAP
CLAP
CLAP
CLAP
THANK YOU, NICOLE. AND THANK YOU, ONE AND ALL.
WITHOUT YOU-- THE CONTESTANTS-- WE'D JUST BE FILMING AN EMPTY HOUSE.
HOW BORING WOULD *THAT* BE?

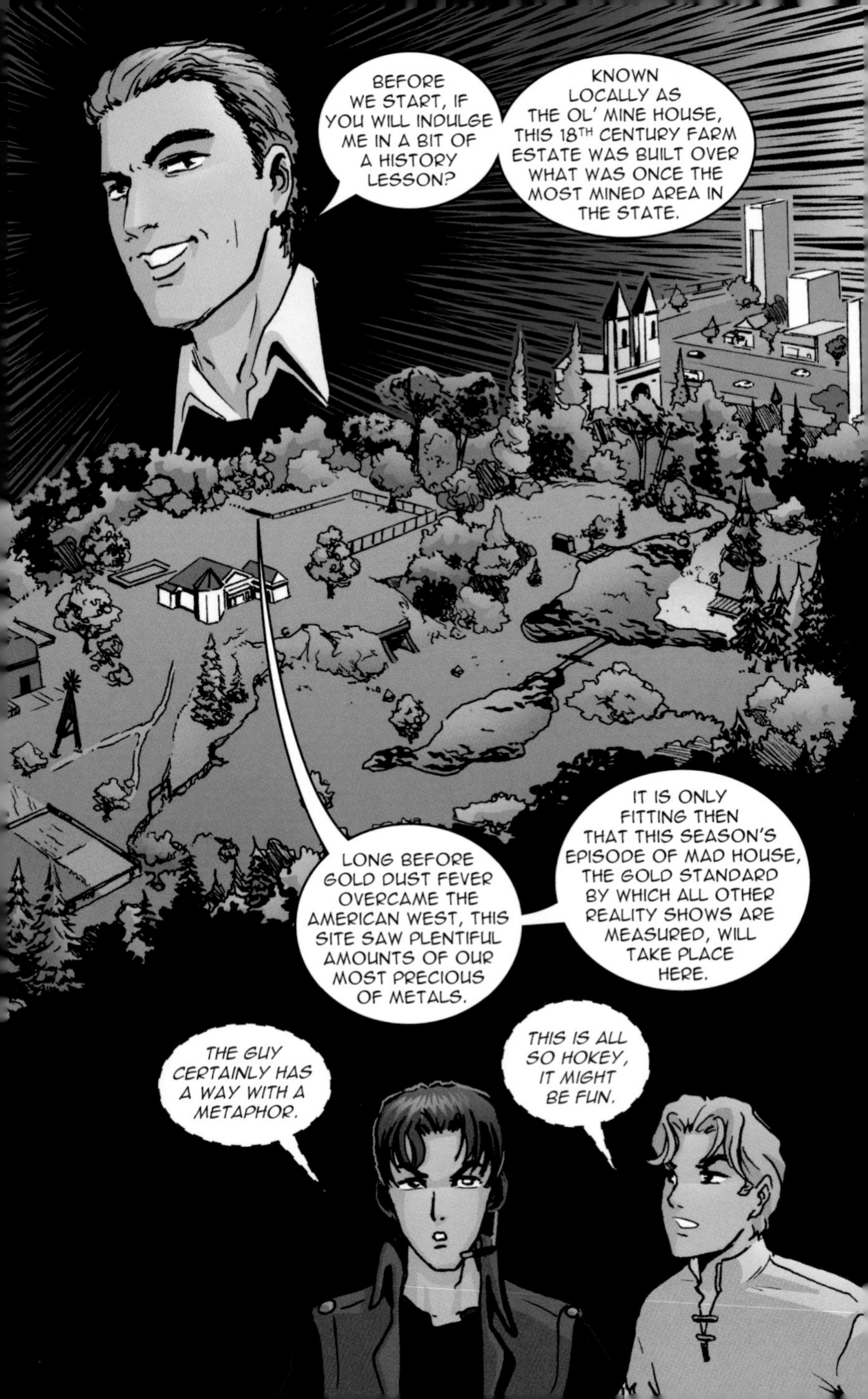
BEFORE WE START, IF YOU WILL INDULGE ME IN A BIT OF A HISTORY LESSON?
KNOWN LOCALLY AS THE OL' MINE HOUSE, THIS 18TH CENTURY FARM ESTATE WAS BUILT OVER WHAT WAS ONCE THE MOST MINED AREA IN THE STATE.
LONG BEFORE GOLD DUST FEVER OVERCAME THE AMERICAN WEST, THIS SITE SAW PLENTIFUL AMOUNTS OF OUR MOST PRECIOUS OF METALS.
IT IS ONLY FITTING THEN THAT THIS SEASON'S EPISODE OF MAD HOUSE, THE GOLD STANDARD BY WHICH ALL OTHER REALITY SHOWS ARE MEASURED, WILL TAKE PLACE HERE.
THE GUY CERTAINLY HAS A WAY WITH A METAPHOR.
THIS IS ALL SO HOKEY, IT MIGHT BE FUN.

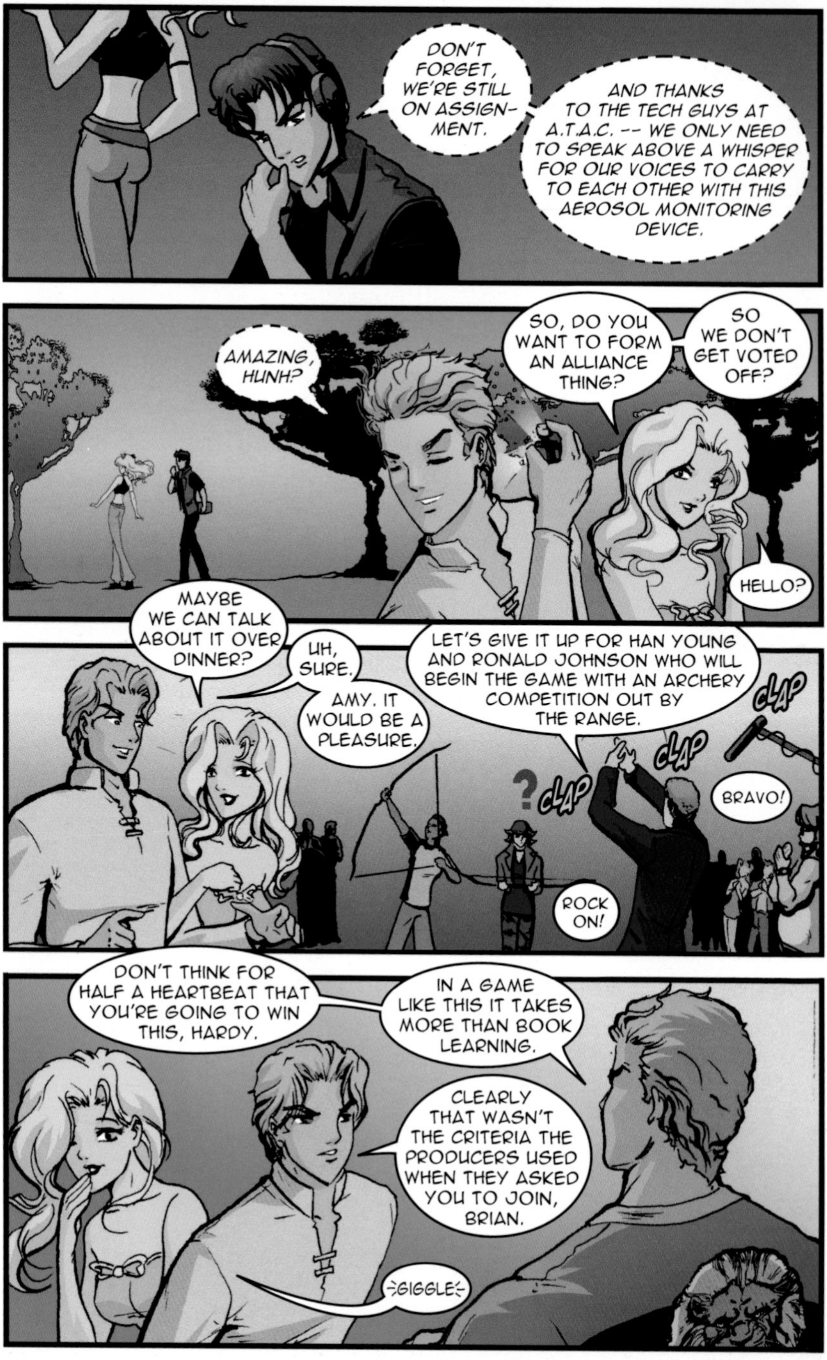
DON'T FORGET, WE'RE STILL ON ASSIGN-MENT.
AND THANKS TO THE TECH GUYS AT A.T.A.C. -- WE ONLY NEED TO SPEAK ABOVE A WHISPER FOR OUR VOICES TO CARRY TO EACH OTHER WITH THIS AEROSOL MONITORING DEVICE.
AMAZING, HUNH?
SO, DO YOU WANT TO FORM AN ALLIANCE THING?
SO WE DON'T GET VOTED OFF?
HELLO?
MAYBE WE CAN TALK ABOUT IT OVER DINNER?
UH, SURE.
AMY. IT WOULD BE A PLEASURE.
LET'S GIVE IT UP FOR HAN YOUNG AND RONALD JOHNSON WHO WILL BEGIN THE GAME WITH AN ARCHERY COMPETITION OUT BY THE RANGE.
CLAP
CLAP
?
CLAP
BRAVO!
ROCK ON!
DON'T THINK FOR HALF A HEARTBEAT THAT YOU'RE GOING TO WIN THIS, HARDY.
IN A GAME LIKE THIS IT TAKES MORE THAN BOOK LEARNING.
CLEARLY THAT WASN'T THE CRITERIA THE PRODUCERS USED WHEN THEY ASKED YOU TO JOIN, BRIAN.
GIGGLE

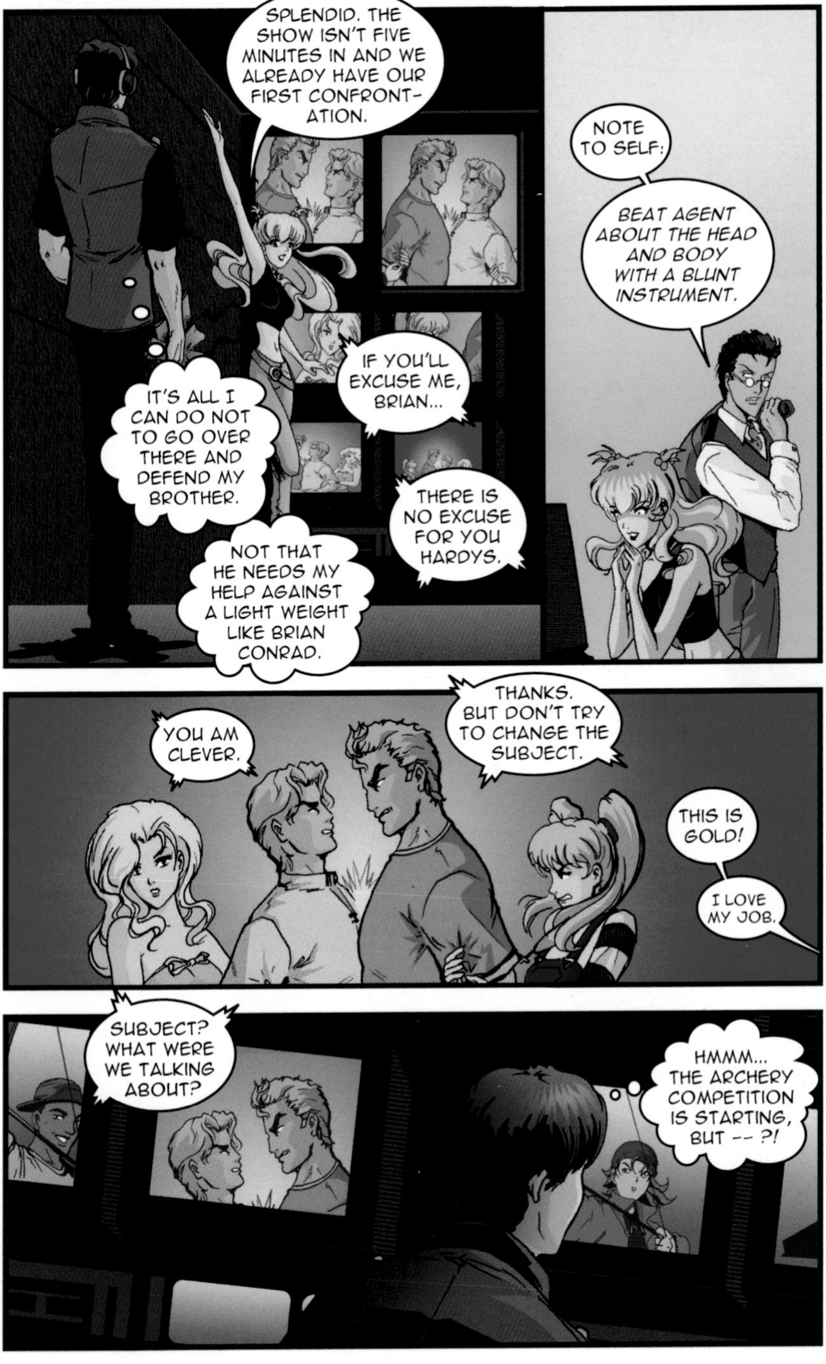
SPLENDID. THE SHOW ISN'T FIVE MINUTES IN AND WE ALREADY HAVE OUR FIRST CONFRONT-ATION.
NOTE TO SELF:
BEAT AGENT ABOUT THE HEAD AND BODY WITH A BLUNT INSTRUMENT.
IT'S ALL I CAN DO NOT TO GO OVER THERE AND DEFEND MY BROTHER.
IF YOU'LL EXCUSE ME, BRIAN...
THERE IS NO EXCUSE FOR YOU HARDYS.
NOT THAT HE NEEDS MY HELP AGAINST A LIGHT WEIGHT LIKE BRIAN CONRAD.
YOU AM CLEVER.
THANKS. BUT DON'T TRY TO CHANGE THE SUBJECT.
THIS IS GOLD!
I LOVE MY JOB.
SUBJECT? WHAT WERE WE TALKING ABOUT?
HMMM... THE ARCHERY COMPETITION IS STARTING, BUT -- ?!

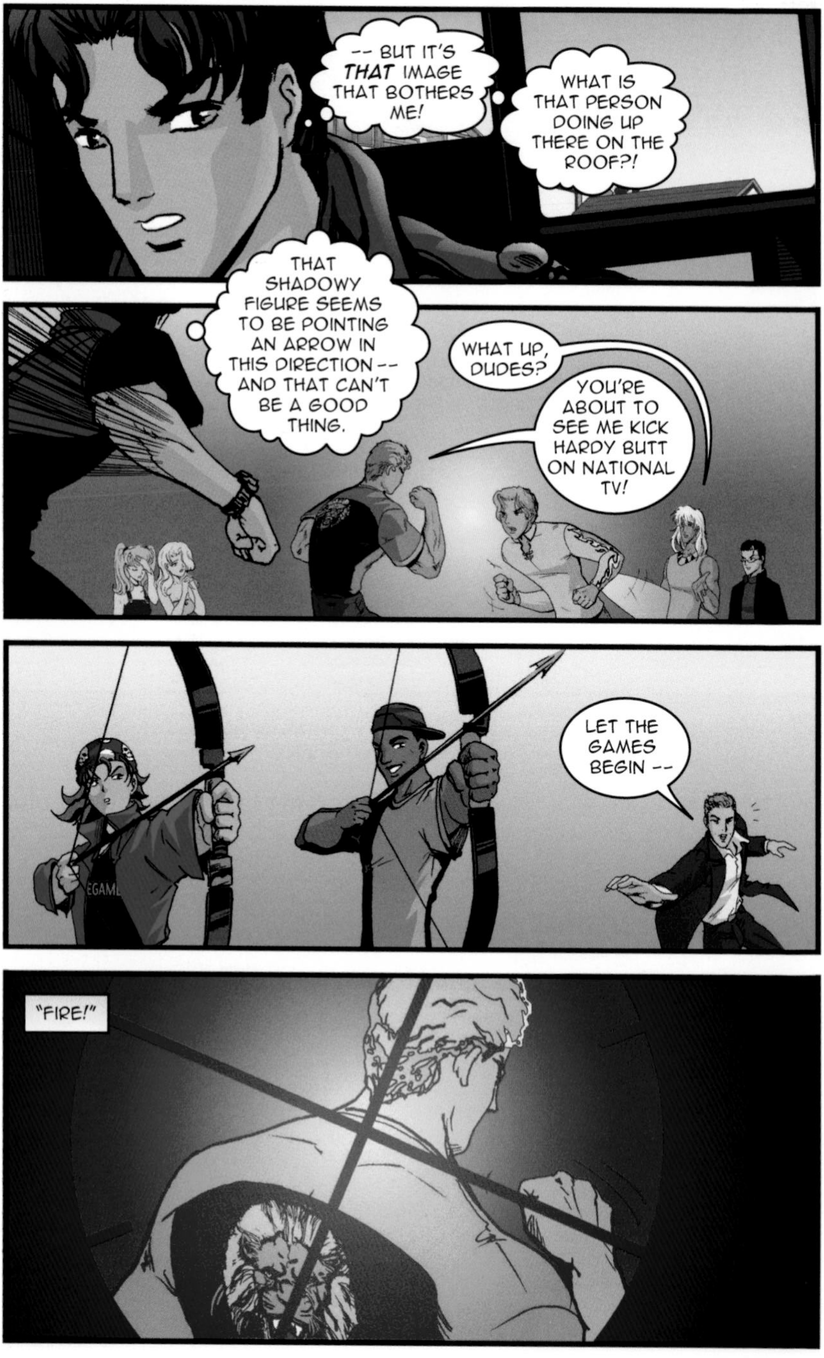
-- BUT IT'S *THAT* IMAGE THAT BOTHERS ME!
WHAT IS THAT PERSON DOING UP THERE ON THE ROOF?!
THAT SHADOWY FIGURE SEEMS TO BE POINTING AN ARROW IN THIS DIRECTION -- AND THAT CAN'T BE A GOOD THING.
WHAT UP, DUDES?
YOU'RE ABOUT TO SEE ME KICK HARDY BUTT ON NATIONAL TV!
LET THE GAMES BEGIN --
"FIRE!"

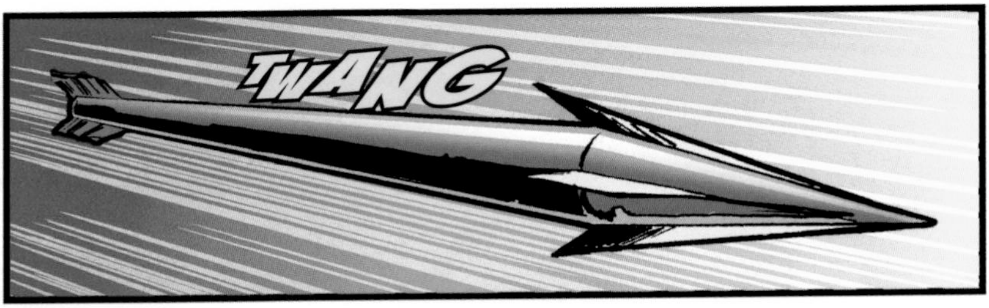
TWANG

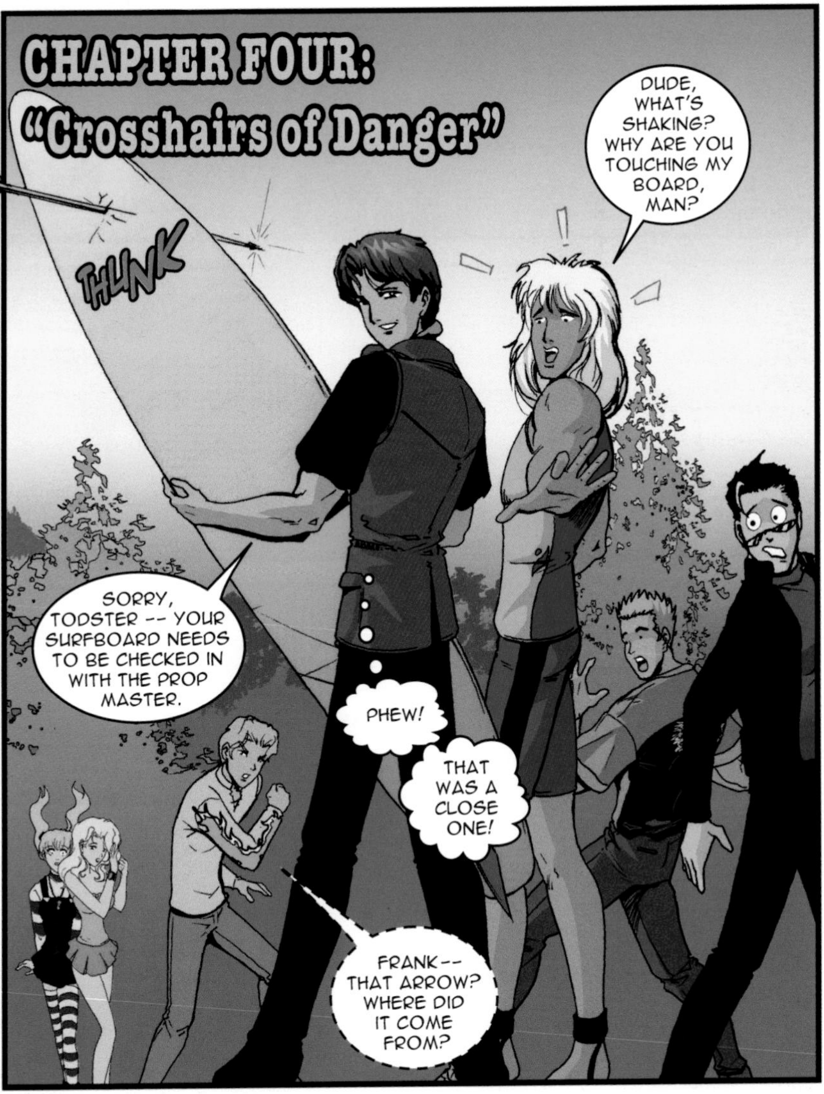
CHAPTER FOUR:
"Crosshairs of Danger"
THUNK
DUDE, WHAT'S SHAKING? WHY ARE YOU TOUCHING MY BOARD, MAN?
SORRY, TODSTER -- YOUR SURFBOARD NEEDS TO BE CHECKED IN WITH THE PROP MASTER.
PHEW!
THAT WAS A CLOSE ONE!
FRANK-- THAT ARROW? WHERE DID IT COME FROM?

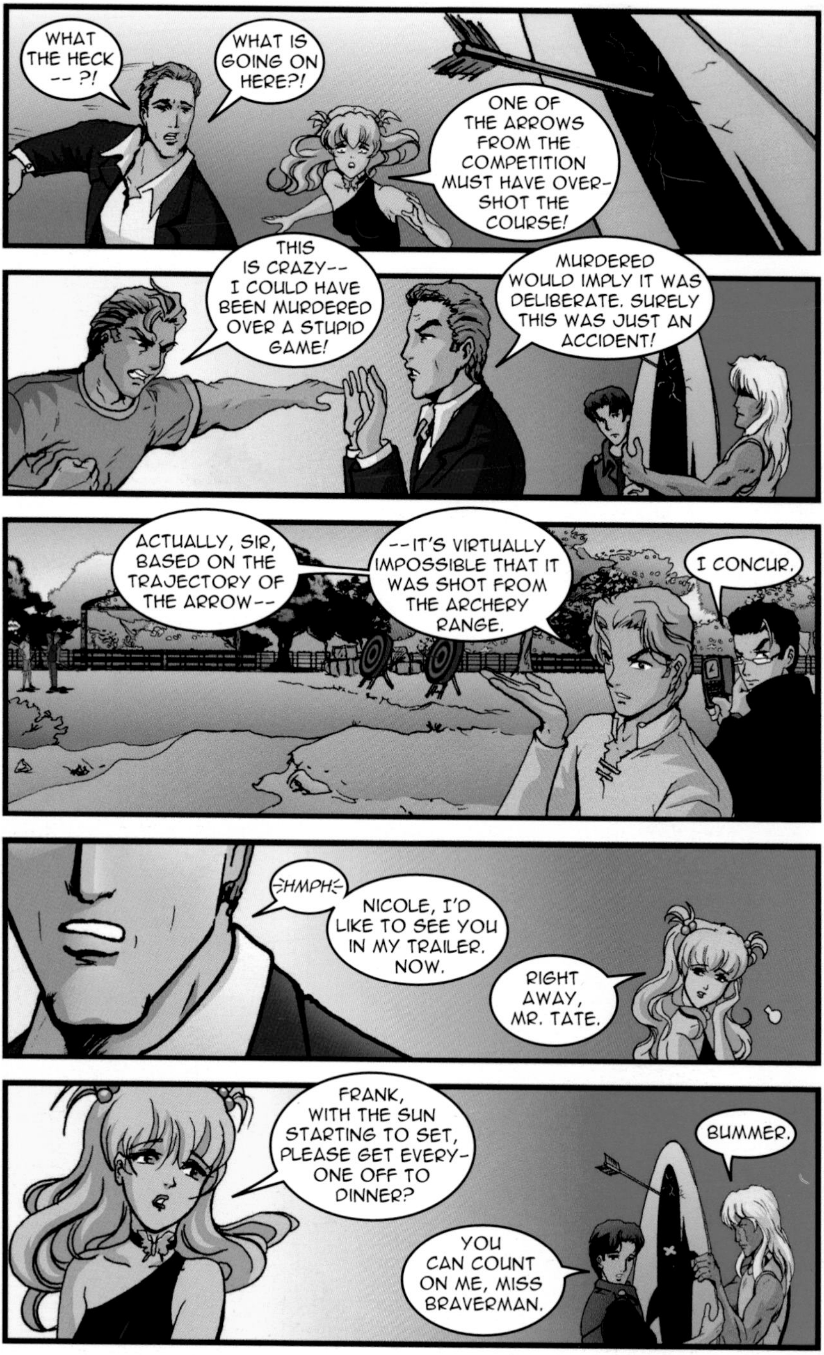
WHAT THE HECK -- ?!
WHAT IS GOING ON HERE?!
ONE OF THE ARROWS FROM THE COMPETITION MUST HAVE OVER-SHOT THE COURSE!
THIS IS CRAZY-- I COULD HAVE BEEN MURDERED OVER A STUPID GAME!
MURDERED WOULD IMPLY IT WAS DELIBERATE. SURELY THIS WAS JUST AN ACCIDENT!
ACTUALLY, SIR, BASED ON THE TRAJECTORY OF THE ARROW--
--IT'S VIRTUALLY IMPOSSIBLE THAT IT WAS SHOT FROM THE ARCHERY RANGE.
I CONCUR.
HMPH
NICOLE, I'D LIKE TO SEE YOU IN MY TRAILER. NOW.
RIGHT AWAY, MR. TATE.
FRANK, WITH THE SUN STARTING TO SET, PLEASE GET EVERY-ONE OFF TO DINNER?
BUMMER.
YOU CAN COUNT ON ME, MISS BRAVERMAN.

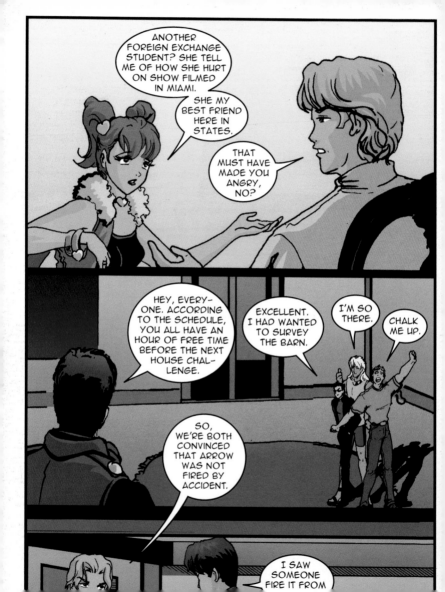

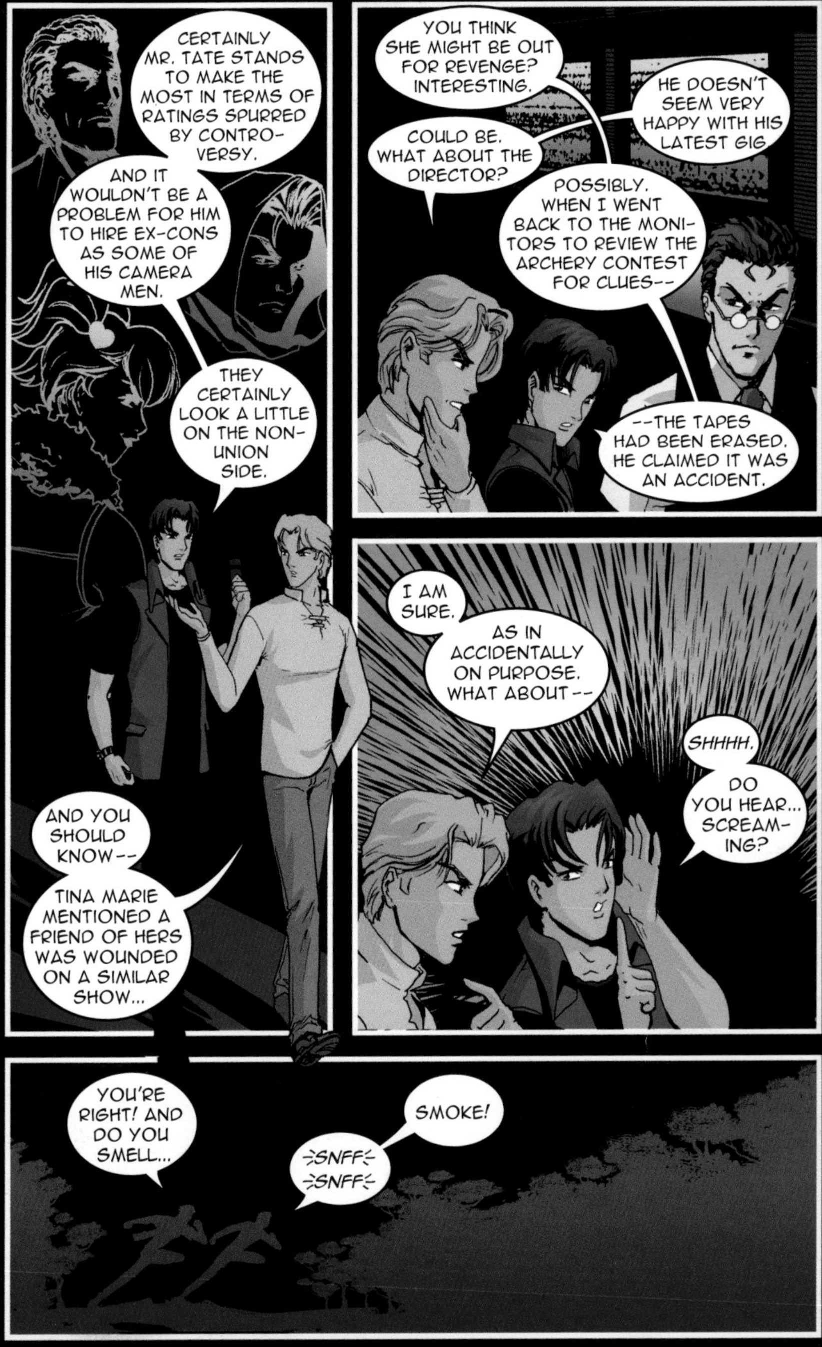
CERTAINLY MR. TATE STANDS TO MAKE THE MOST IN TERMS OF RATINGS SPURRED BY CONTRO-VERSY.
AND IT WOULDN'T BE A PROBLEM FOR HIM TO HIRE EX-CONS AS SOME OF HIS CAMERA MEN.
THEY CERTAINLY LOOK A LITTLE ON THE NON-UNION SIDE.
AND YOU SHOULD KNOW--
TINA MARIE MENTIONED A FRIEND OF HERS WAS WOUNDED ON A SIMILAR SHOW...
YOU THINK SHE MIGHT BE OUT FOR REVENGE? INTERESTING.
COULD BE. WHAT ABOUT THE DIRECTOR?
HE DOESN'T SEEM VERY HAPPY WITH HIS LATEST GIG
POSSIBLY. WHEN I WENT BACK TO THE MONI-TORS TO REVIEW THE ARCHERY CONTEST FOR CLUES--
--THE TAPES HAD BEEN ERASED. HE CLAIMED IT WAS AN ACCIDENT.
I AM SURE.
AS IN ACCIDENTALLY ON PURPOSE. WHAT ABOUT --
SHHHH.
DO YOU HEAR... SCREAM-ING?
YOU'RE RIGHT! AND DO YOU SMELL...
SNFF SNFF
SMOKE!

CHAPTER FIVE: "The Heat is On!"

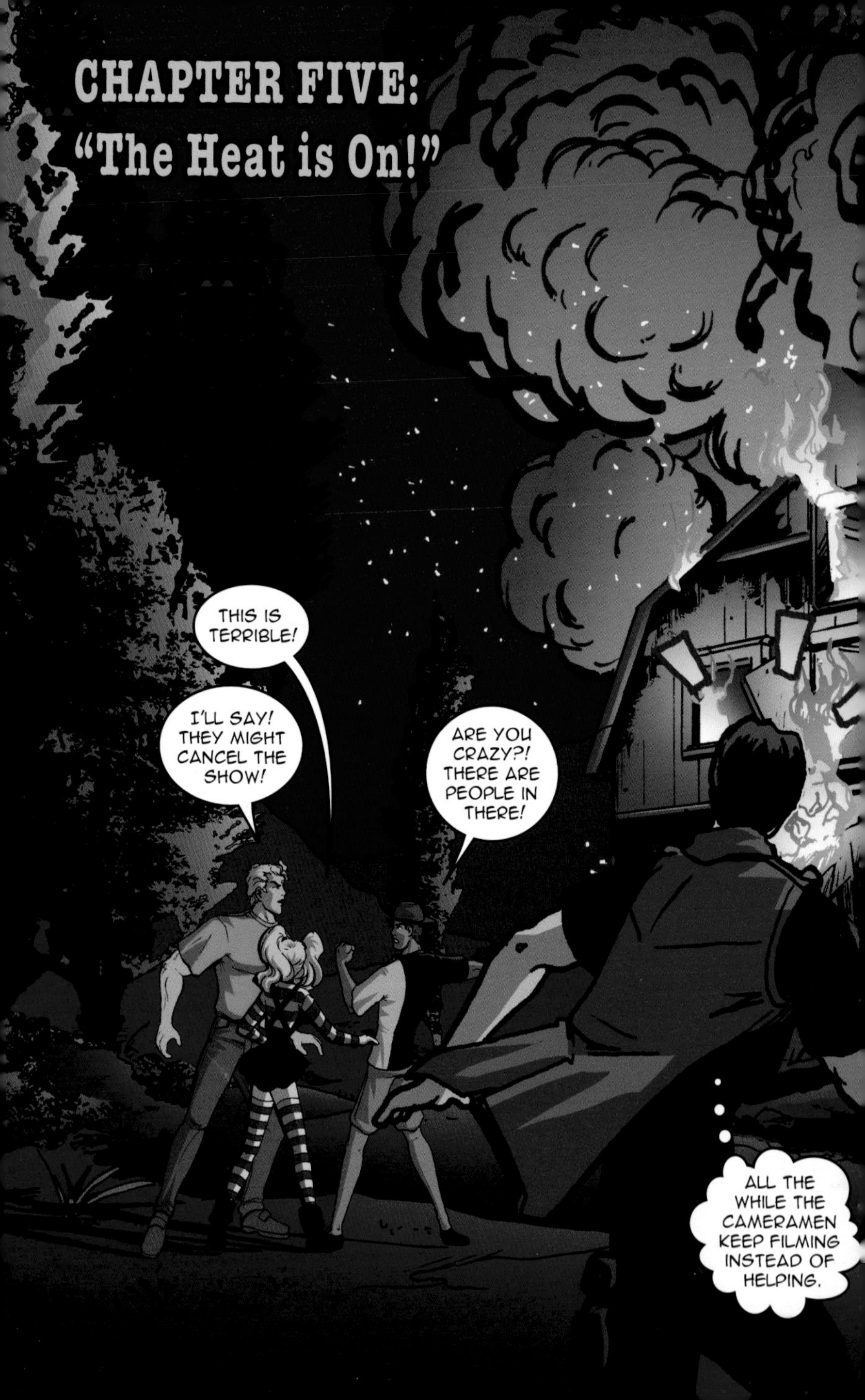

THIS IS TERRIBLE!
I'LL SAY! THEY MIGHT CANCEL THE SHOW!
ARE YOU CRAZY?! THERE ARE PEOPLE IN THERE!
ALL THE WHILE THE CAMERAMEN KEEP FILMING INSTEAD OF HELPING.

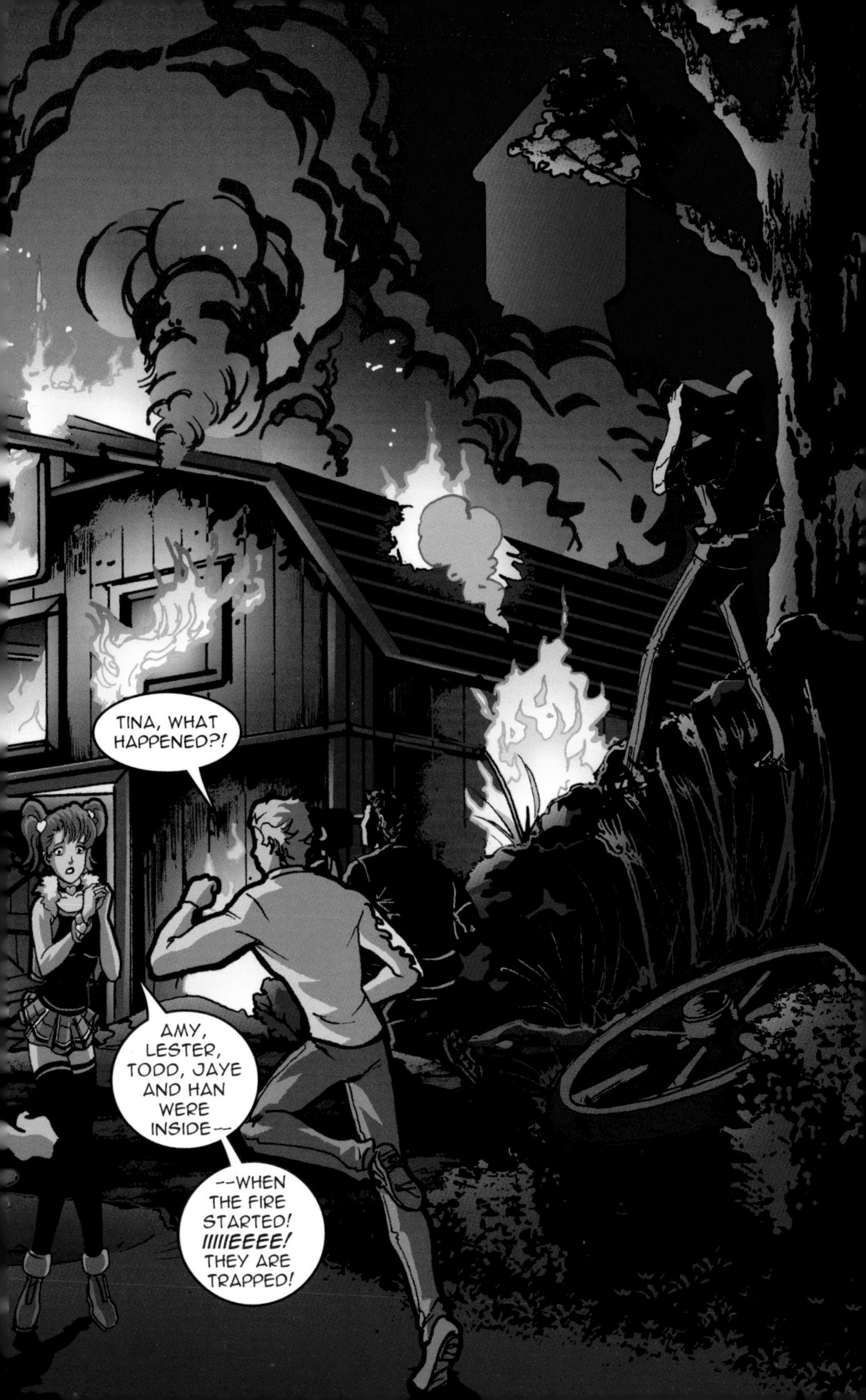
TINA, WHAT HAPPENED?!
AMY, LESTER, TODD, JAYE AND HAN WERE INSIDE--
--WHEN THE FIRE STARTED! IIIIIEEEE! THEY ARE TRAPPED!

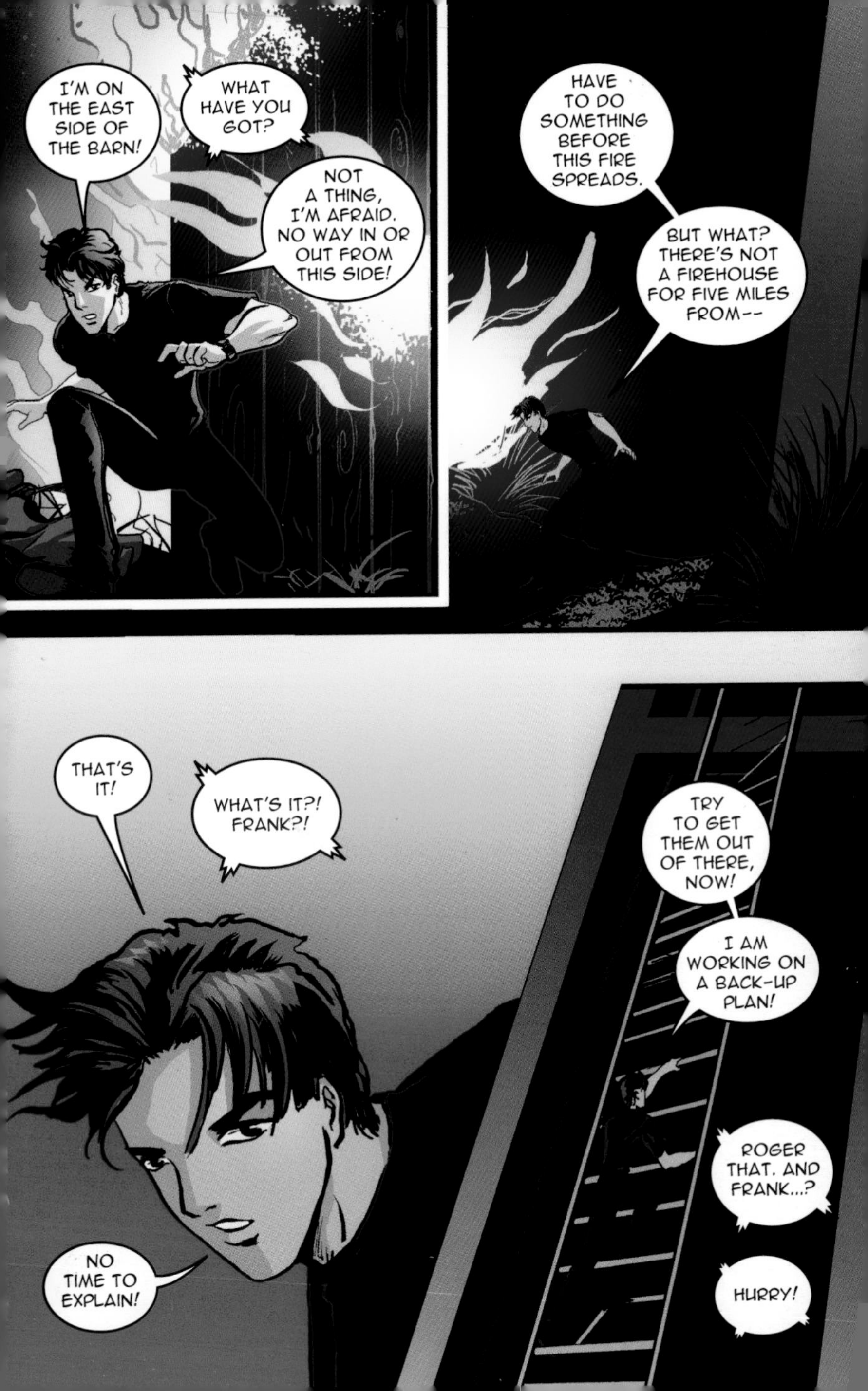
I'M ON THE EAST SIDE OF THE BARN!
WHAT HAVE YOU GOT?
NOT A THING, I'M AFRAID. NO WAY IN OR OUT FROM THIS SIDE!
HAVE TO DO SOMETHING BEFORE THIS FIRE SPREADS.
BUT WHAT? THERE'S NOT A FIREHOUSE FOR FIVE MILES FROM--
THAT'S IT!
WHAT'S IT?! FRANK?!
NO TIME TO EXPLAIN!
TRY TO GET THEM OUT OF THERE, NOW!
I AM WORKING ON A BACK-UP PLAN!
ROGER THAT. AND FRANK...?
HURRY!

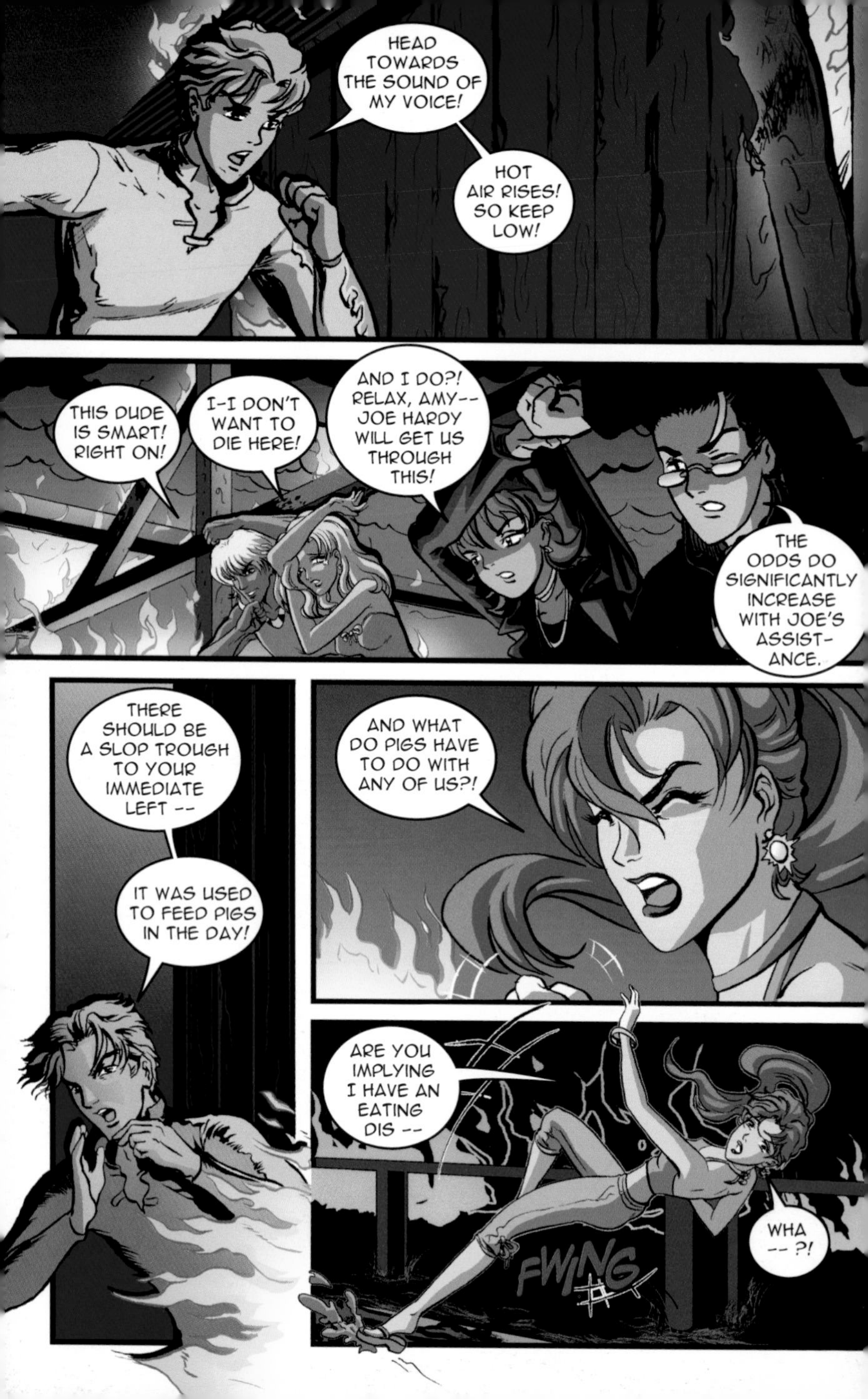
HEAD TOWARDS THE SOUND OF MY VOICE!
HOT AIR RISES! SO KEEP LOW!
THIS DUDE IS SMART! RIGHT ON!
I-I DON'T WANT TO DIE HERE!
AND I DO?! RELAX, AMY-- JOE HARDY WILL GET US THROUGH THIS!
THE ODDS DO SIGNIFICANTLY INCREASE WITH JOE'S ASSIST-ANCE.
THERE SHOULD BE A SLOP TROUGH TO YOUR IMMEDIATE LEFT --
IT WAS USED TO FEED PIGS IN THE DAY!
AND WHAT DO PIGS HAVE TO DO WITH ANY OF US?!
ARE YOU IMPLYING I HAVE AN EATING DIS --
WHA -- ?!
FWING

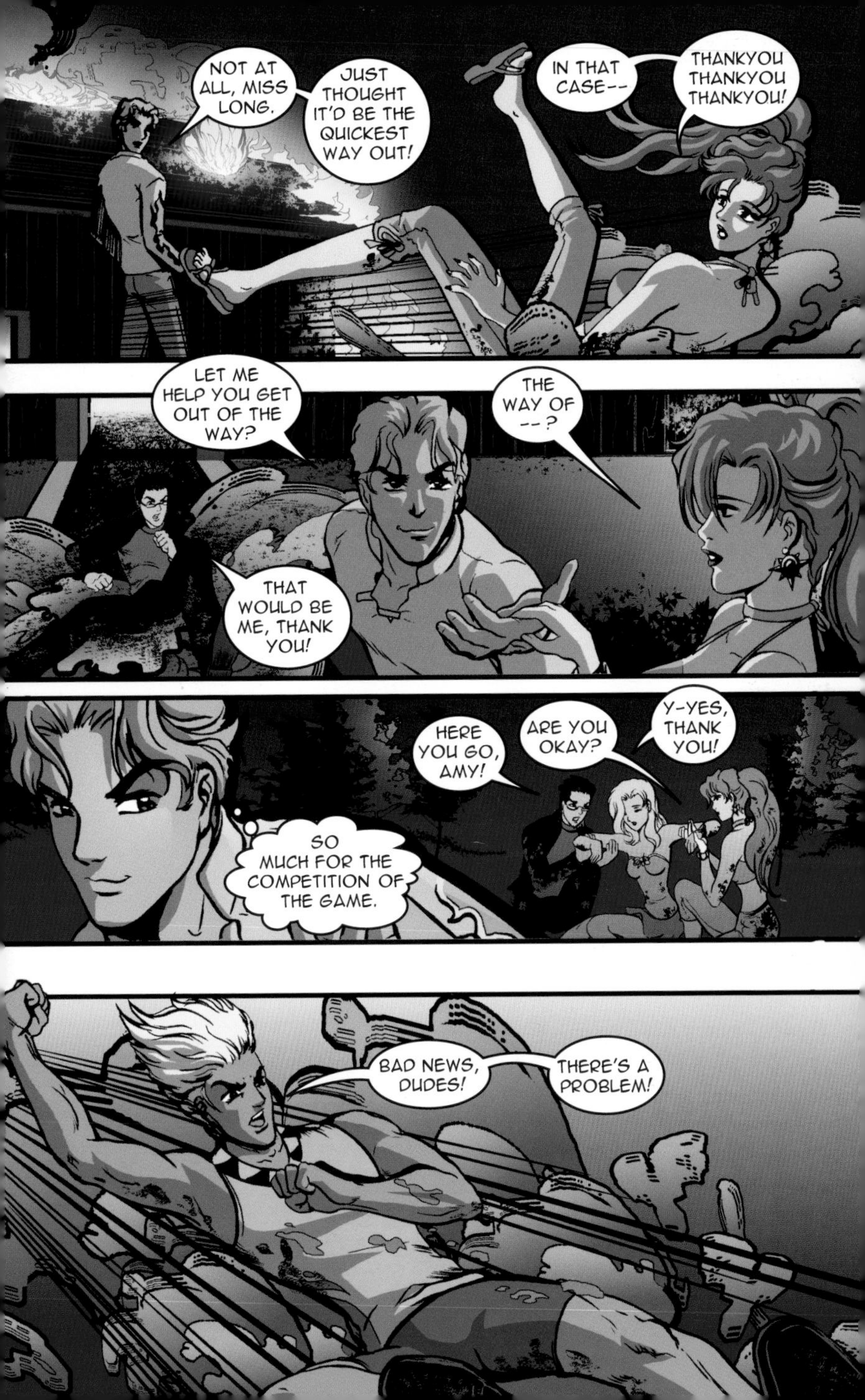
NOT AT ALL, MISS LONG.
JUST THOUGHT IT'D BE THE QUICKEST WAY OUT!
IN THAT CASE--
THANKYOU THANKYOU THANKYOU!
LET ME HELP YOU GET OUT OF THE WAY?
THE WAY OF --?
THAT WOULD BE ME, THANK YOU!
HERE YOU GO, AMY!
ARE YOU OKAY?
Y-YES, THANK YOU!
SO MUCH FOR THE COMPETITION OF THE GAME.
BAD NEWS, DUDES!
THERE'S A PROBLEM!

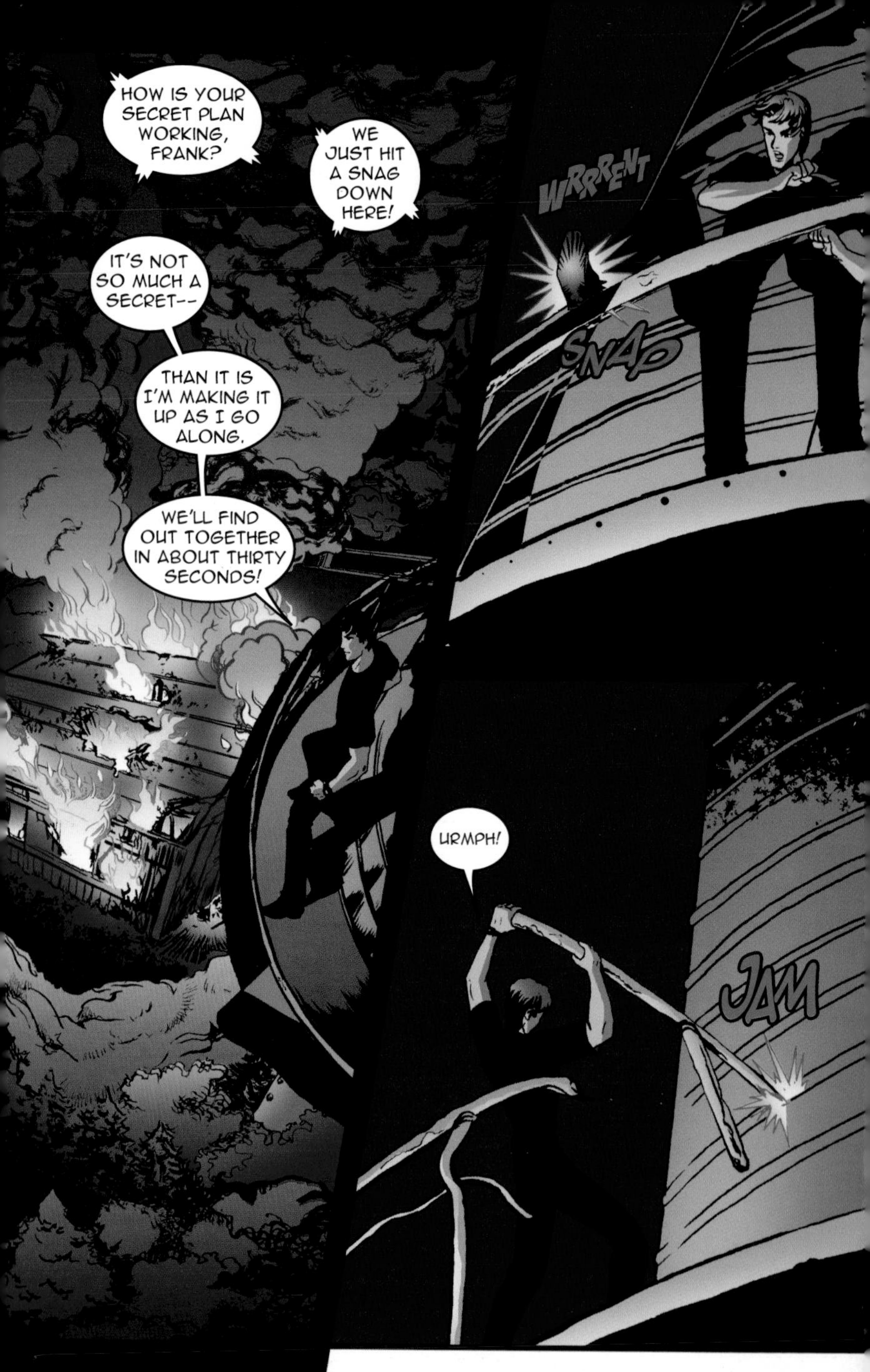
HOW IS YOUR SECRET PLAN WORKING, FRANK?
WE JUST HIT A SNAG DOWN HERE!
WIRRRENT
IT'S NOT SO MUCH A SECRET--
SNAP
THAN IT IS I'M MAKING IT UP AS I GO ALONG.
WE'LL FIND OUT TOGETHER IN ABOUT THIRTY SECONDS!
URMPH!
JAM

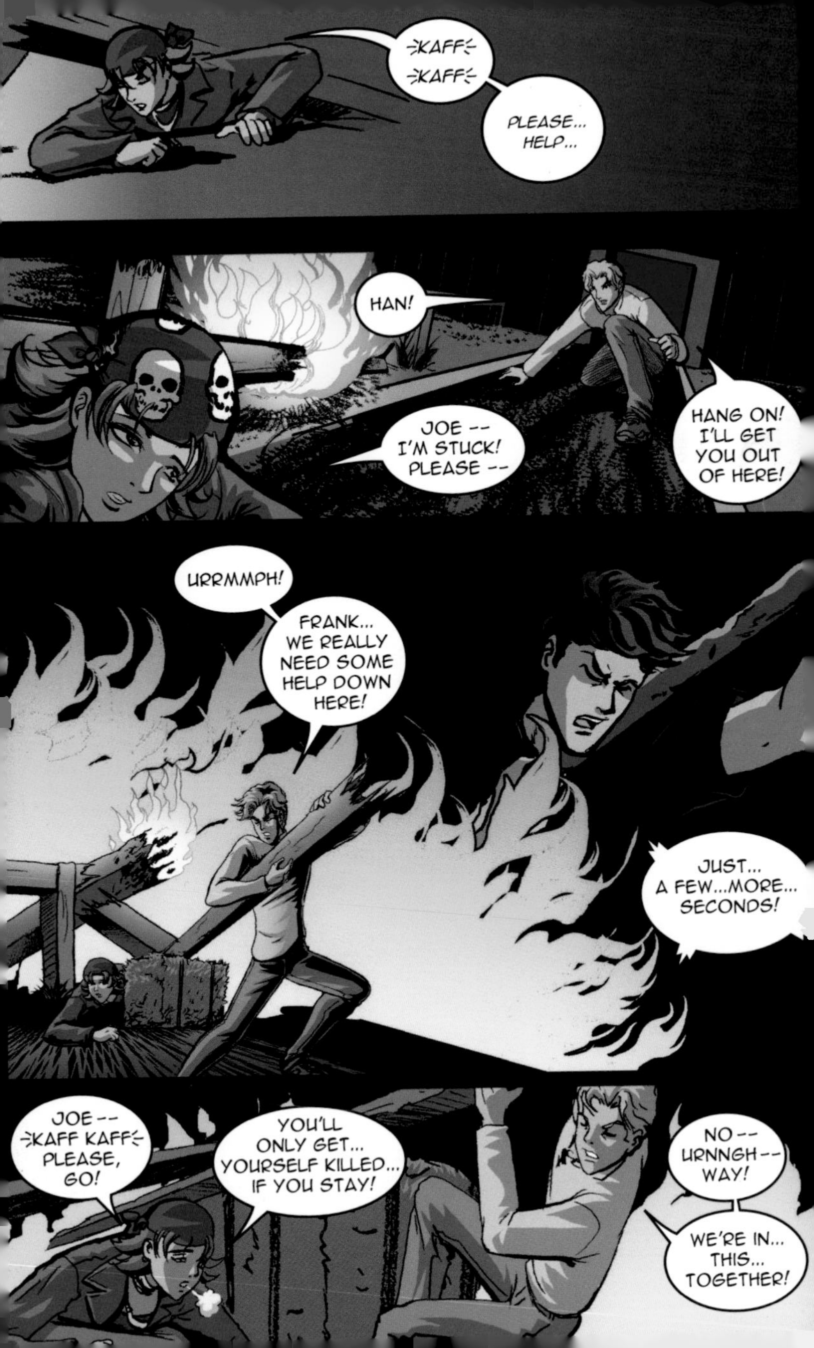

-KAFF-
-KAFF-
PLEASE... HELP...
HAN!
JOE -- I'M STUCK! PLEASE --
HANG ON! I'LL GET YOU OUT OF HERE!
URRMMPH!
FRANK... WE REALLY NEED SOME HELP DOWN HERE!
JUST... A FEW...MORE... SECONDS!
JOE -- -KAFF KAFF- PLEASE, GO!
YOU'LL ONLY GET... YOURSELF KILLED... IF YOU STAY!
NO -- URNNGH -- WAY!
WE'RE IN... THIS... TOGETHER!

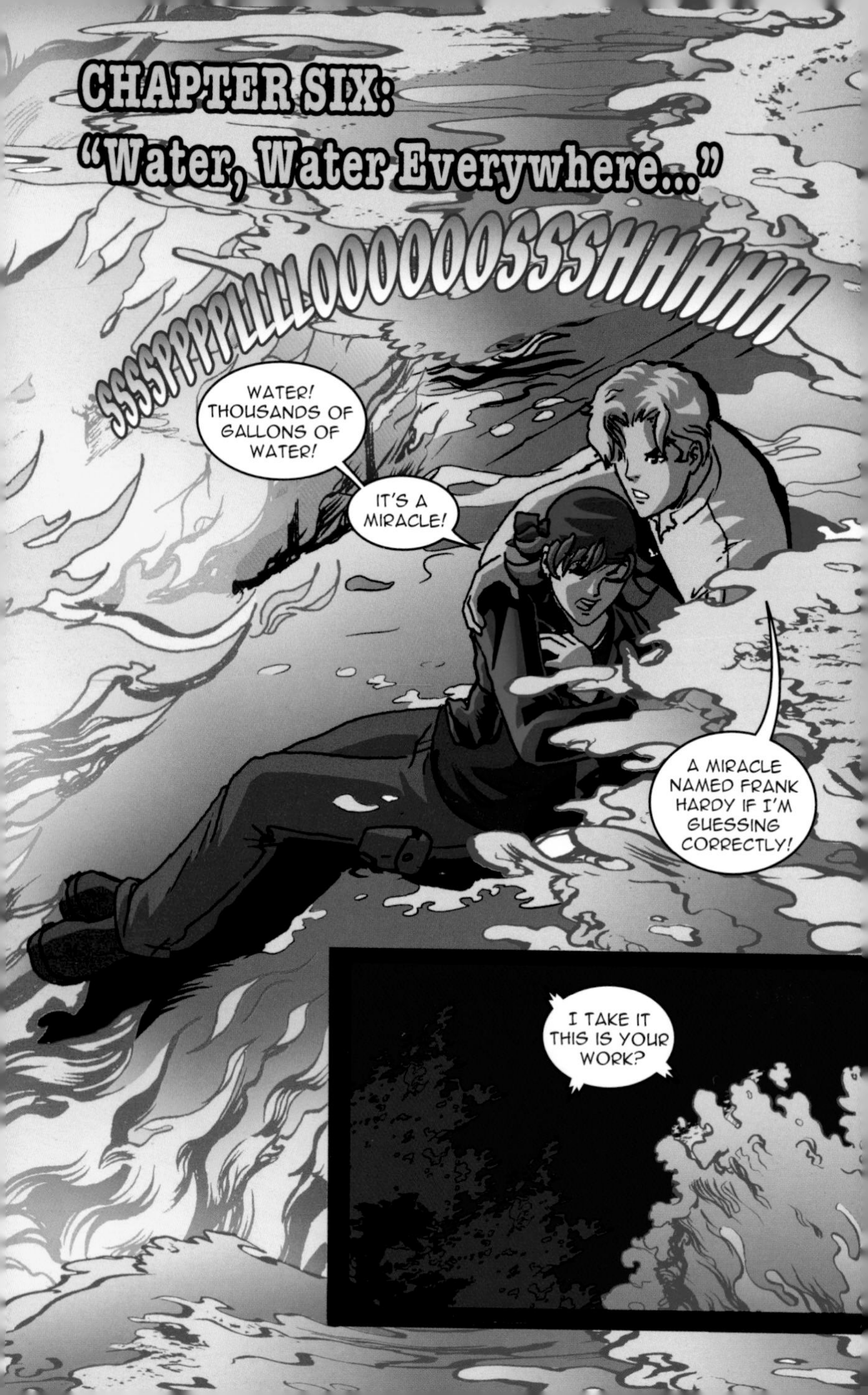
CHAPTER SIX:
"Water, Water Everywhere..."
SSSSPPPPLLLLOOOOOOOSSSSHHHHHH
WATER! THOUSANDS OF GALLONS OF WATER!
IT'S A MIRACLE!
A MIRACLE NAMED FRANK HARDY IF I'M GUESSING CORRECTLY!
I TAKE IT THIS IS YOUR WORK?

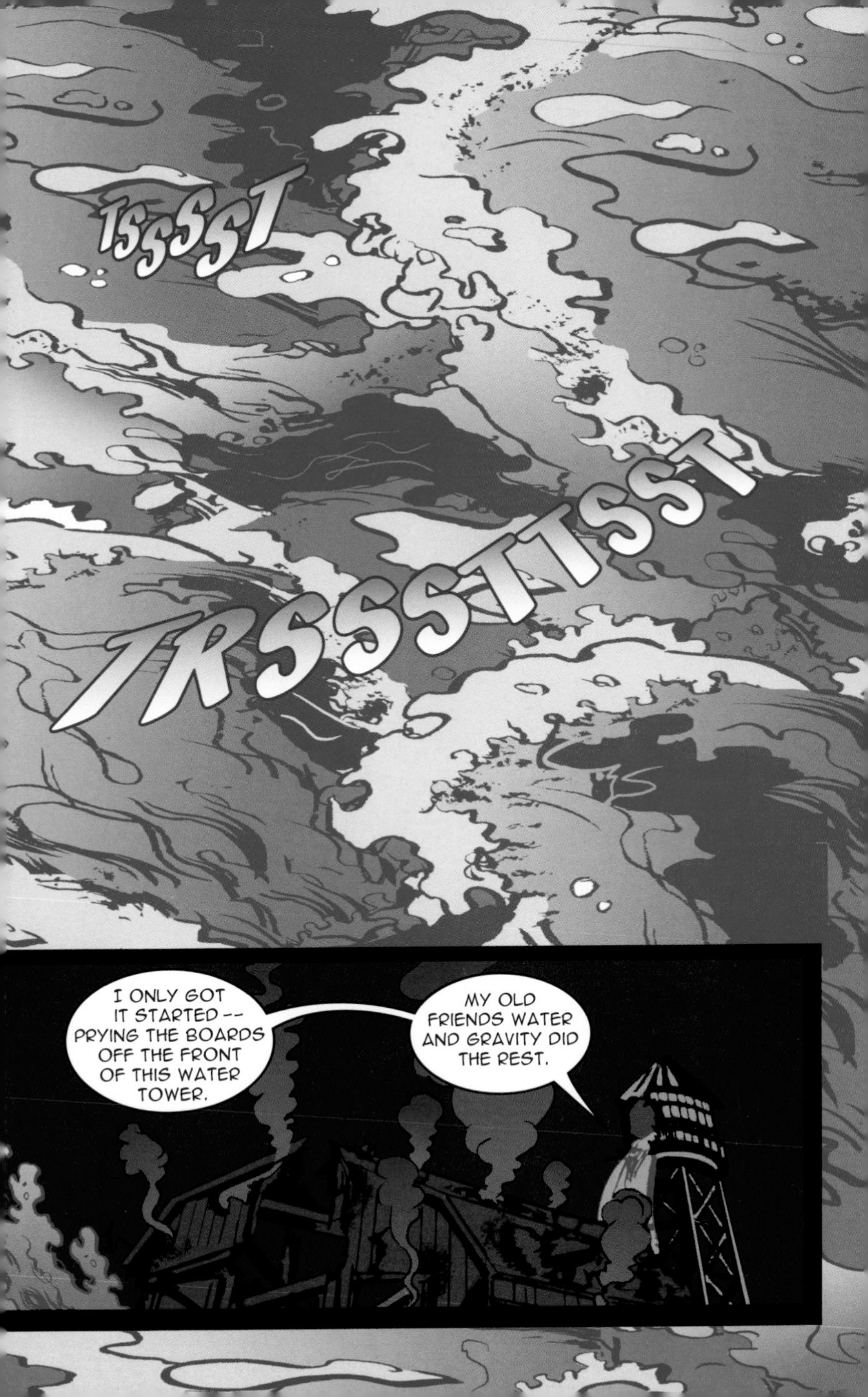
TSSSST
TRSSSTTSST
I ONLY GOT IT STARTED -- PRYING THE BOARDS OFF THE FRONT OF THIS WATER TOWER.
MY OLD FRIENDS WATER AND GRAVITY DID THE REST.

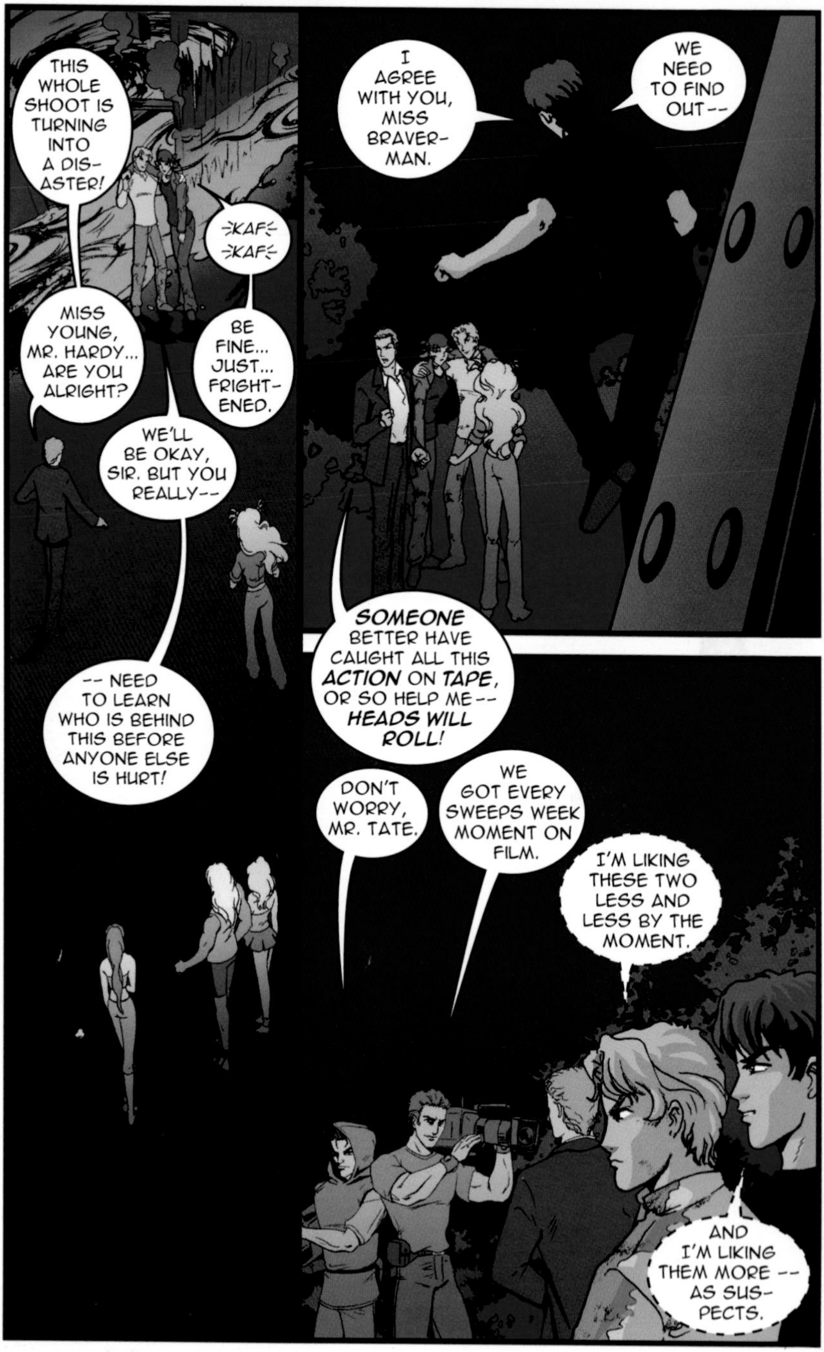
THIS WHOLE SHOOT IS TURNING INTO A DIS-ASTER!
KAF KAF
MISS YOUNG, MR. HARDY... ARE YOU ALRIGHT?
BE FINE... JUST... FRIGHT-ENED.
WE'LL BE OKAY, SIR. BUT YOU REALLY--
-- NEED TO LEARN WHO IS BEHIND THIS BEFORE ANYONE ELSE IS HURT!
I AGREE WITH YOU, MISS BRAVER-MAN.
WE NEED TO FIND OUT--
SOMEONE BETTER HAVE CAUGHT ALL THIS ACTION ON TAPE, OR SO HELP ME-- HEADS WILL ROLL!
DON'T WORRY, MR. TATE.
WE GOT EVERY SWEEPS WEEK MOMENT ON FILM.
I'M LIKING THESE TWO LESS AND LESS BY THE MOMENT.
AND I'M LIKING THEM MORE -- AS SUS-PECTS.

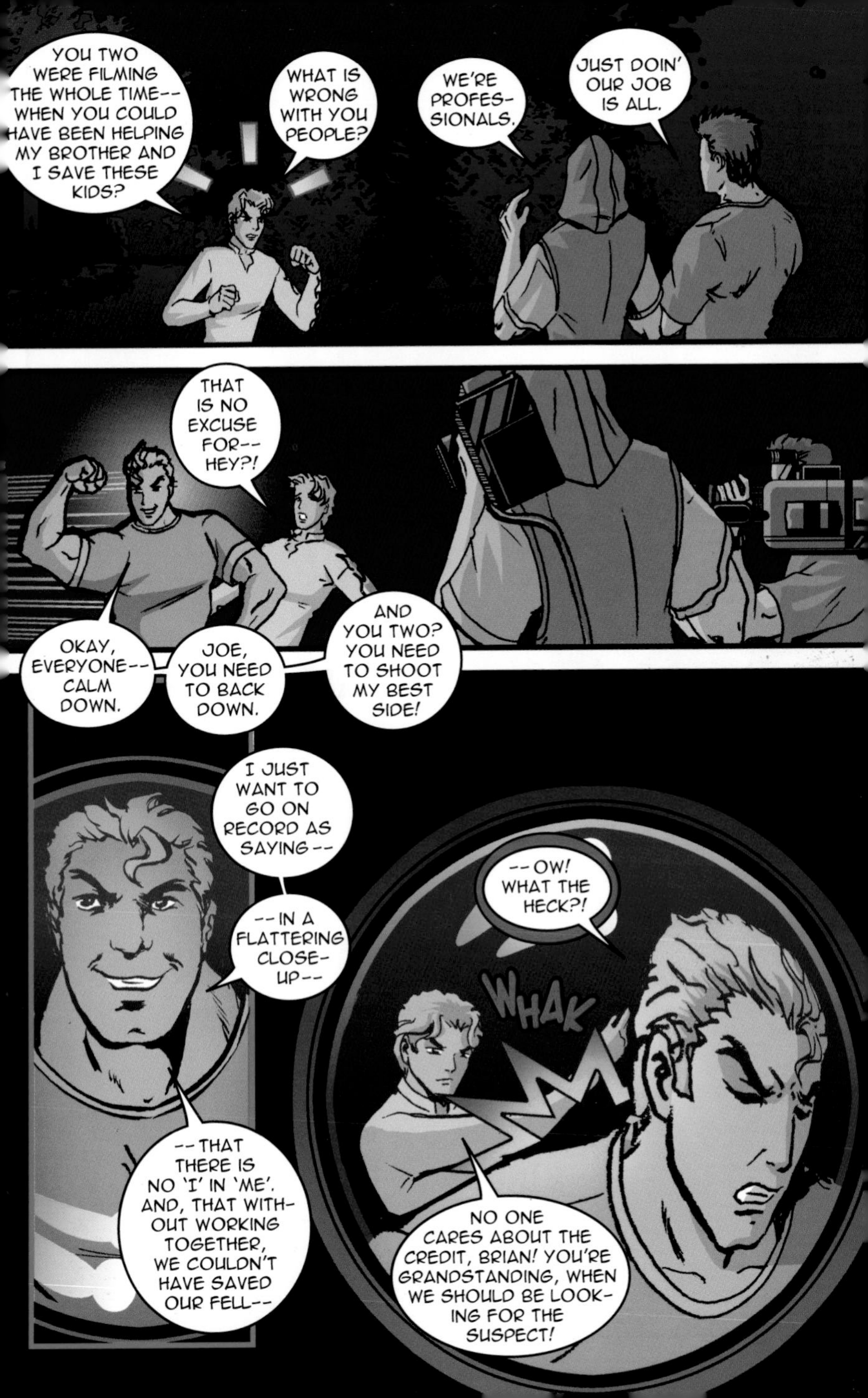
YOU TWO WERE FILMING THE WHOLE TIME-- WHEN YOU COULD HAVE BEEN HELPING MY BROTHER AND I SAVE THESE KIDS?
WHAT IS WRONG WITH YOU PEOPLE?
WE'RE PROFES-SIONALS.
JUST DOIN' OUR JOB IS ALL.
THAT IS NO EXCUSE FOR-- HEY?!
OKAY, EVERYONE-- CALM DOWN.
JOE, YOU NEED TO BACK DOWN.
AND YOU TWO? YOU NEED TO SHOOT MY BEST SIDE!
I JUST WANT TO GO ON RECORD AS SAYING--
--IN A FLATTERING CLOSE-UP--
--THAT THERE IS NO 'I' IN 'ME'. AND, THAT WITH-OUT WORKING TOGETHER, WE COULDN'T HAVE SAVED OUR FELL--
--OW! WHAT THE HECK?!
WHAK
NO ONE CARES ABOUT THE CREDIT, BRIAN! YOU'RE GRANDSTANDING, WHEN WE SHOULD BE LOOK-ING FOR THE SUSPECT!

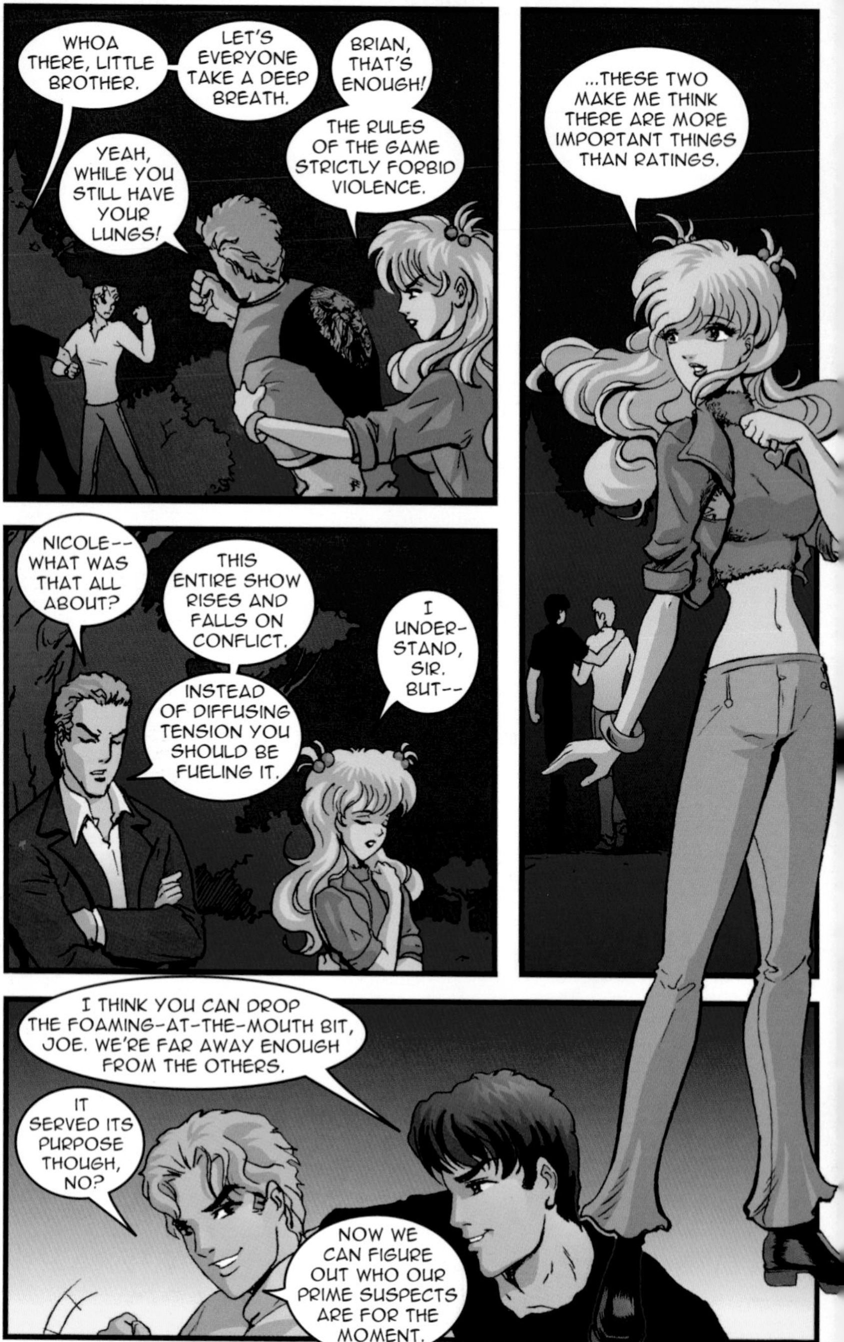
WHOA THERE, LITTLE BROTHER.
LET'S EVERYONE TAKE A DEEP BREATH.
YEAH, WHILE YOU STILL HAVE YOUR LUNGS!
BRIAN, THAT'S ENOUGH!
THE RULES OF THE GAME STRICTLY FORBID VIOLENCE.
NICOLE-- WHAT WAS THAT ALL ABOUT?
THIS ENTIRE SHOW RISES AND FALLS ON CONFLICT.
INSTEAD OF DIFFUSING TENSION YOU SHOULD BE FUELING IT.
I UNDER-STAND, SIR. BUT--
...THESE TWO MAKE ME THINK THERE ARE MORE IMPORTANT THINGS THAN RATINGS.
I THINK YOU CAN DROP THE FOAMING-AT-THE-MOUTH BIT, JOE. WE'RE FAR AWAY ENOUGH FROM THE OTHERS.
IT SERVED ITS PURPOSE THOUGH, NO?
NOW WE CAN FIGURE OUT WHO OUR PRIME SUSPECTS ARE FOR THE MOMENT.

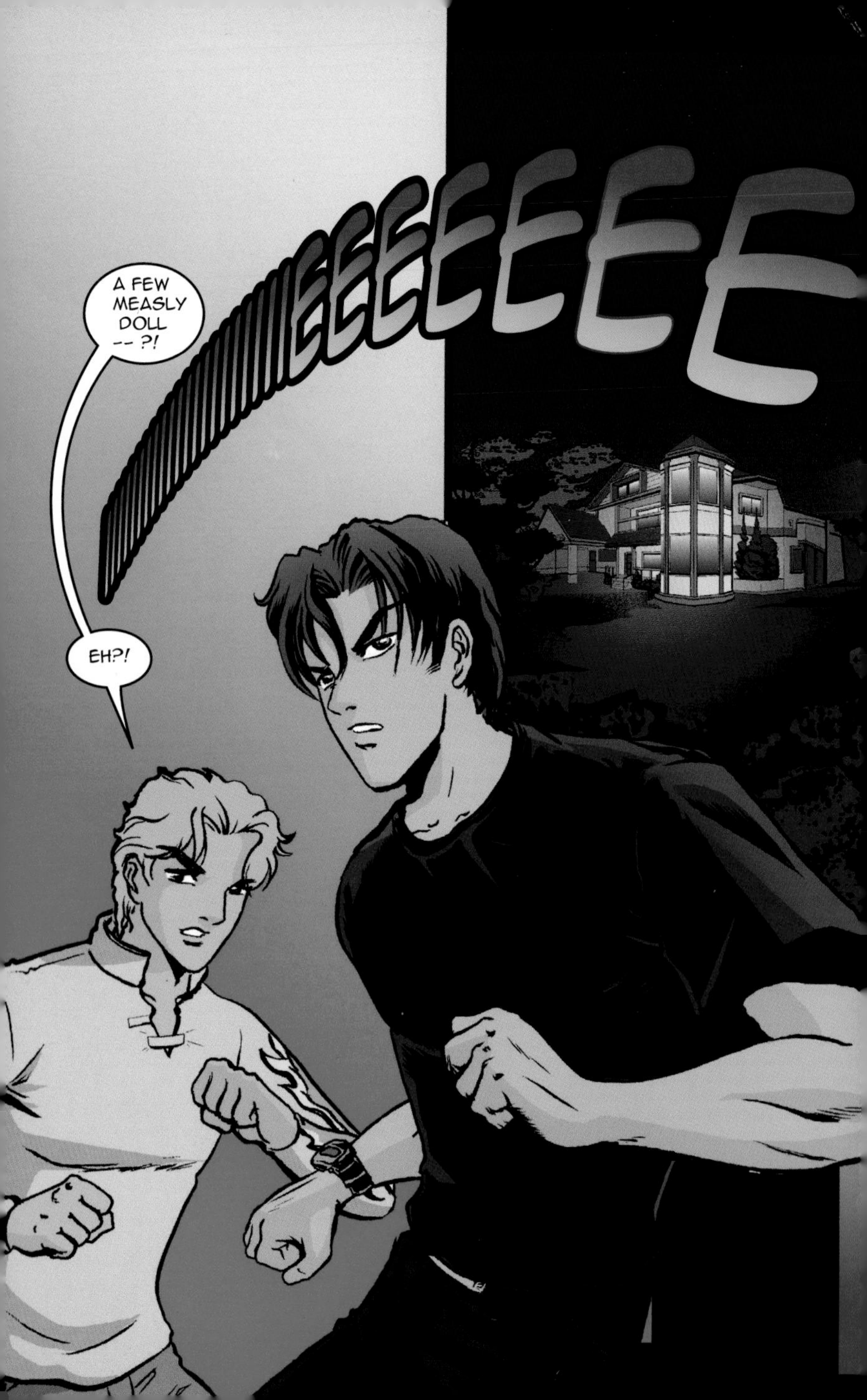

A FEW MEASLY DOLL -- ?!
EH?!
EEEEEEEEEE

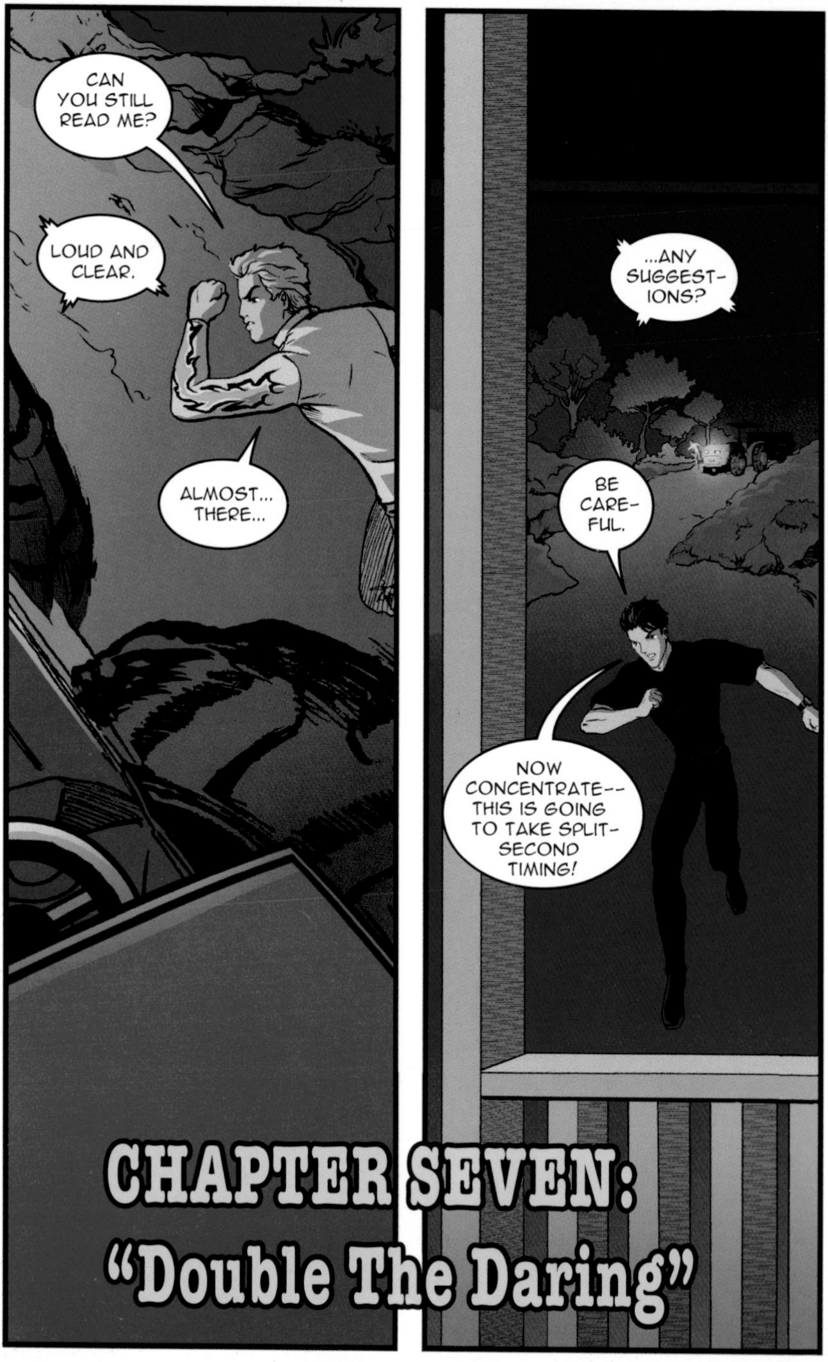
CAN YOU STILL READ ME?
LOUD AND CLEAR.
ALMOST... THERE...
...ANY SUGGEST-IONS?
BE CARE-FUL.
NOW CONCENTRATE-- THIS IS GOING TO TAKE SPLIT-SECOND TIMING!
CHAPTER SEVEN:
"Double The Daring"

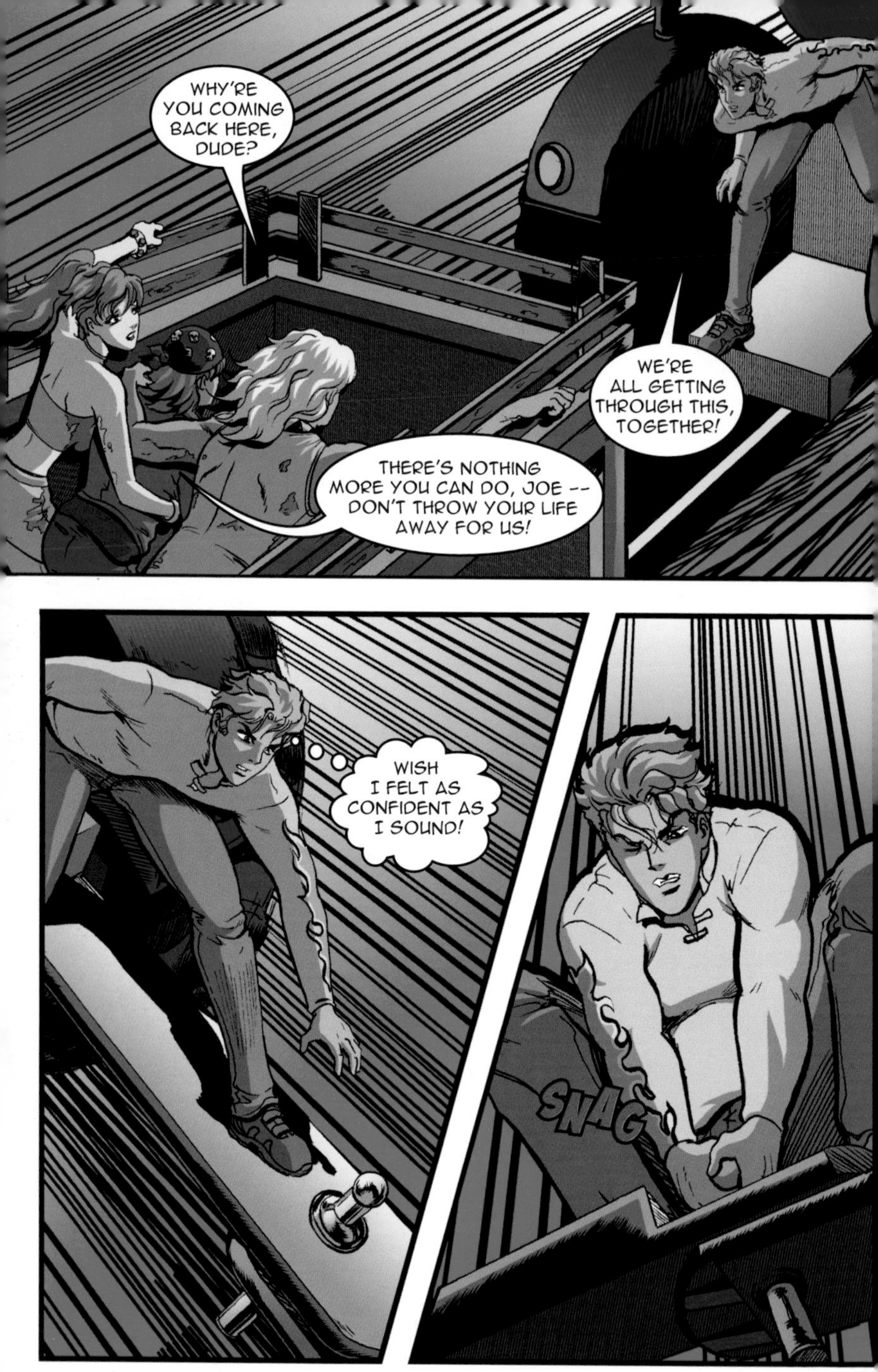
WHY'RE YOU COMING BACK HERE, DUDE?
WE'RE ALL GETTING THROUGH THIS, TOGETHER!
THERE'S NOTHING MORE YOU CAN DO, JOE -- DON'T THROW YOUR LIFE AWAY FOR US!
WISH I FELT AS CONFIDENT AS I SOUND!
SNAG

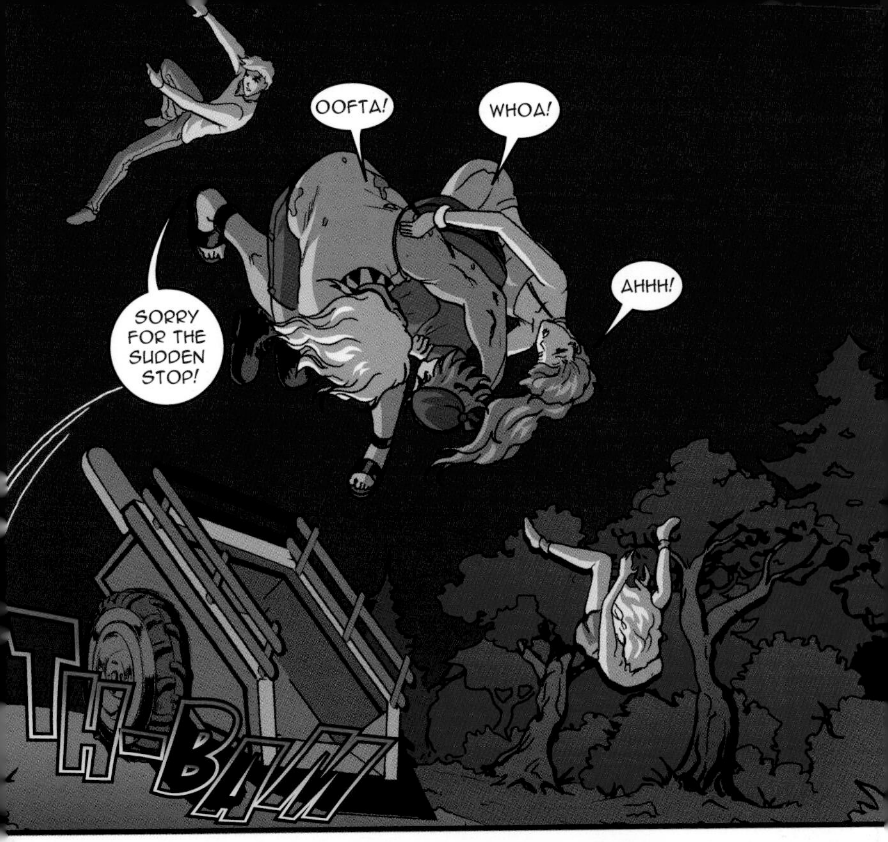
OOFTA!
WHOA!
SORRY FOR THE SUDDEN STOP!
AHHH!
TH-BAM
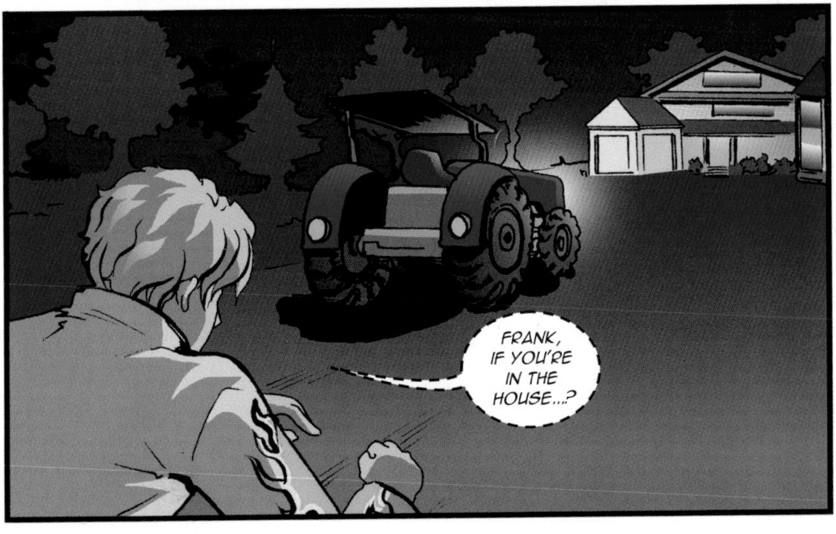
FRANK, IF YOU'RE IN THE HOUSE...?

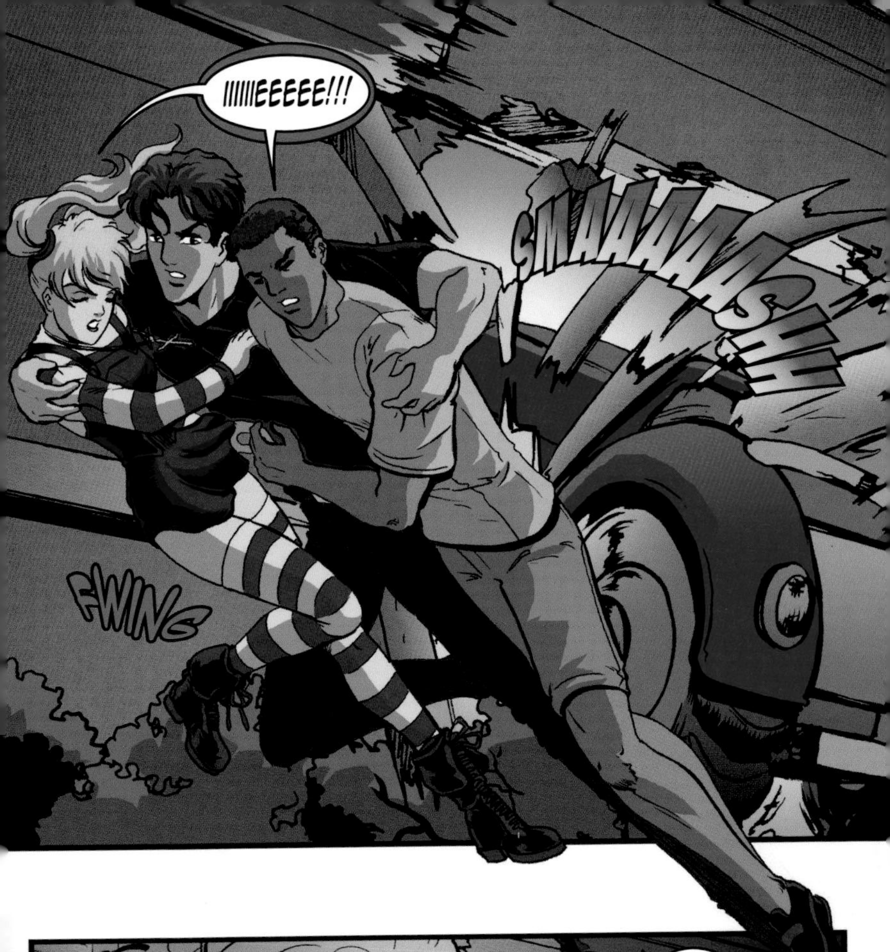
IIIIIIEEEEEE!!!
SMAAAAASHH
FWING

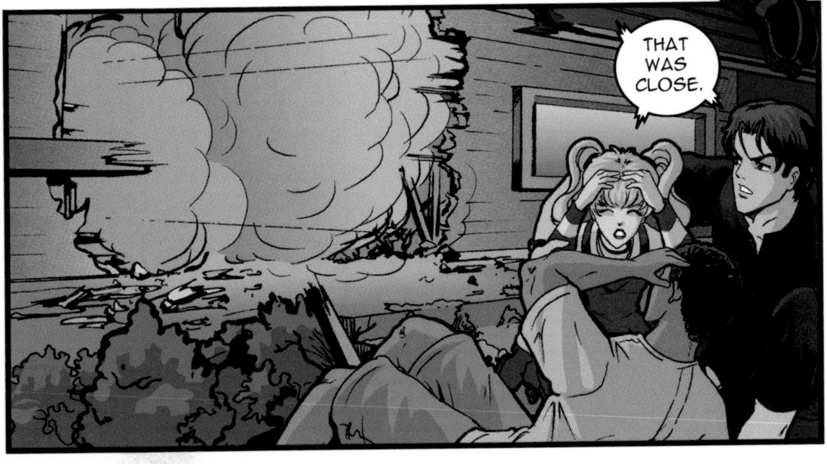
THAT WAS CLOSE.

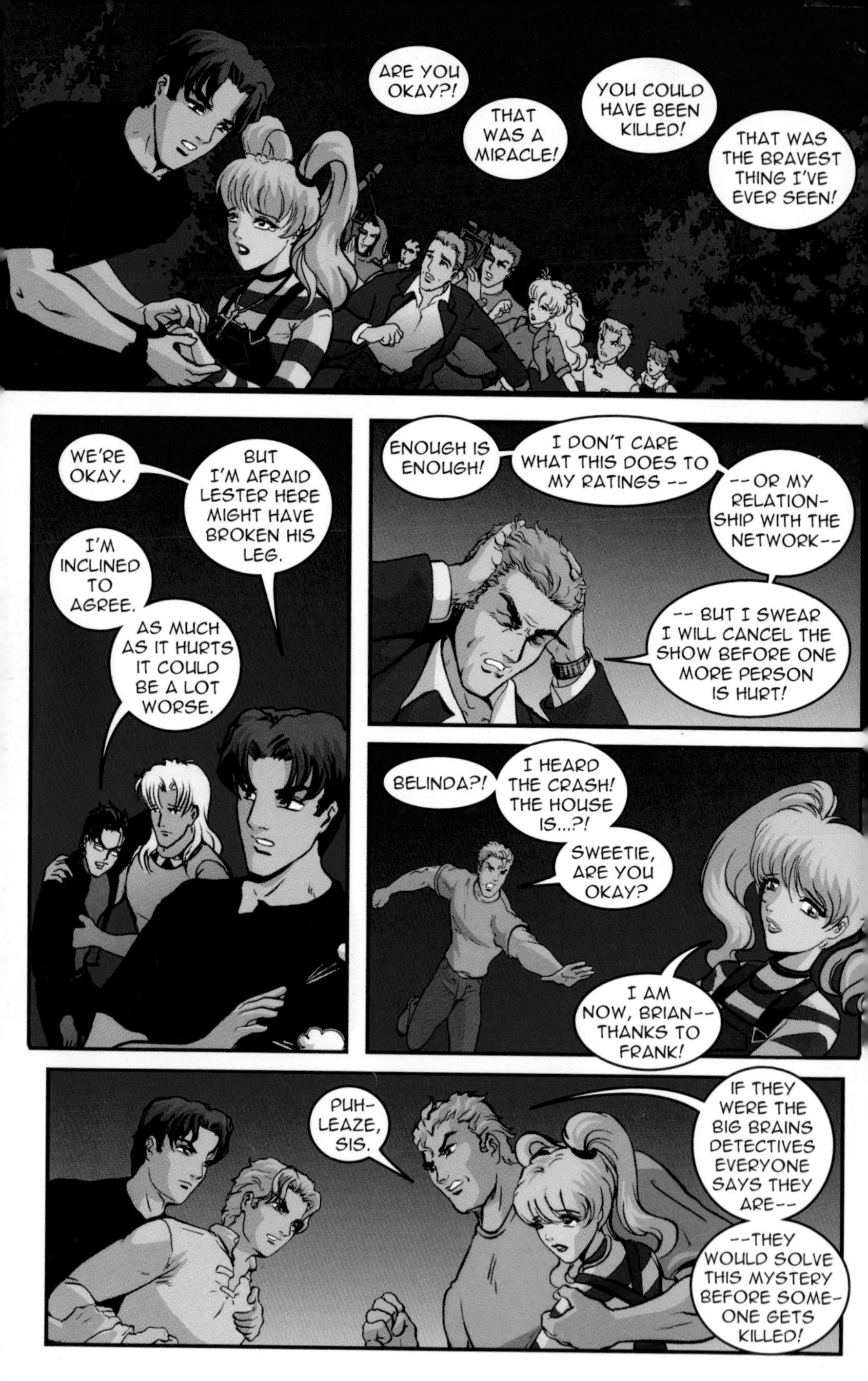
ARE YOU OKAY?!
THAT WAS A MIRACLE!
YOU COULD HAVE BEEN KILLED!
THAT WAS THE BRAVEST THING I'VE EVER SEEN!
WE'RE OKAY.
BUT I'M AFRAID LESTER HERE MIGHT HAVE BROKEN HIS LEG.
I'M INCLINED TO AGREE.
AS MUCH AS IT HURTS IT COULD BE A LOT WORSE.
ENOUGH IS ENOUGH!
I DON'T CARE WHAT THIS DOES TO MY RATINGS --
--OR MY RELATIONSHIP WITH THE NETWORK--
-- BUT I SWEAR I WILL CANCEL THE SHOW BEFORE ONE MORE PERSON IS HURT!
BELINDA?!
I HEARD THE CRASH! THE HOUSE IS...?!
SWEETIE, ARE YOU OKAY?
I AM NOW, BRIAN-- THANKS TO FRANK!
PUH-LEAZE, SIS.
IF THEY WERE THE BIG BRAINS DETECTIVES EVERYONE SAYS THEY ARE--
--THEY WOULD SOLVE THIS MYSTERY BEFORE SOMEONE GETS KILLED!

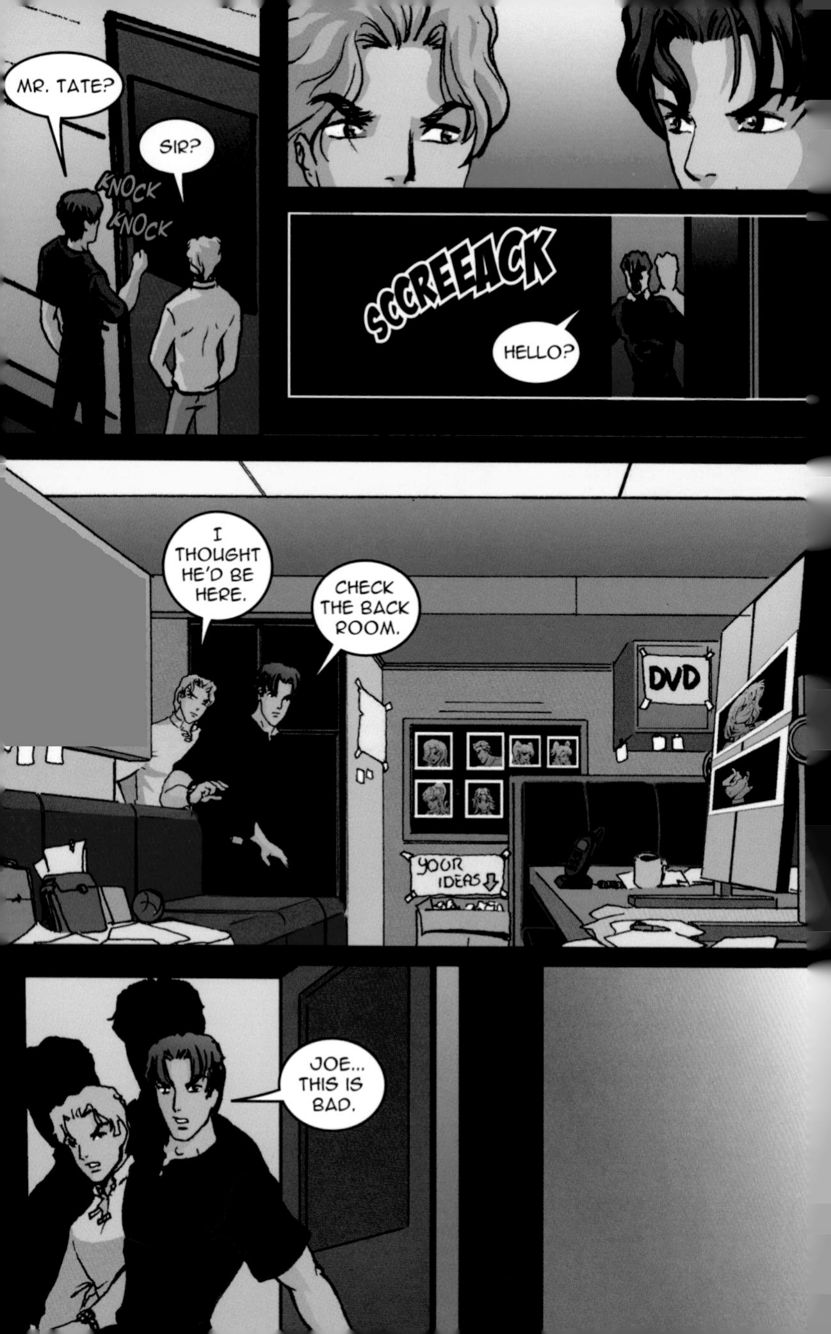
MR. TATE?
KNOCK KNOCK
SIR?
SCCREEACK
HELLO?
I THOUGHT HE'D BE HERE.
CHECK THE BACK ROOM.
DVD
YOUR IDEAS
JOE... THIS IS BAD.

MR. TATE... I-I CAN'T BELIEVE...

I WAS J-JUST...

-- JUST ABOUT TO CALL THE NETWORK, I KNOW.

LET'S STEP OUT HERE AND TALK ABOUT IT.

NOOOO!

MISS BRAVERMAN... I'M SORRY YOU HAD TO SEE THIS.

CHAPTER EIGHT: "Home Farther Away From Home..."

WHAT HAVE YOU GOT?

⇍SNFF⇏
⇍SNFF⇏

SMELLS FAINTLY LIKE ALMONDS. CYANIDE.

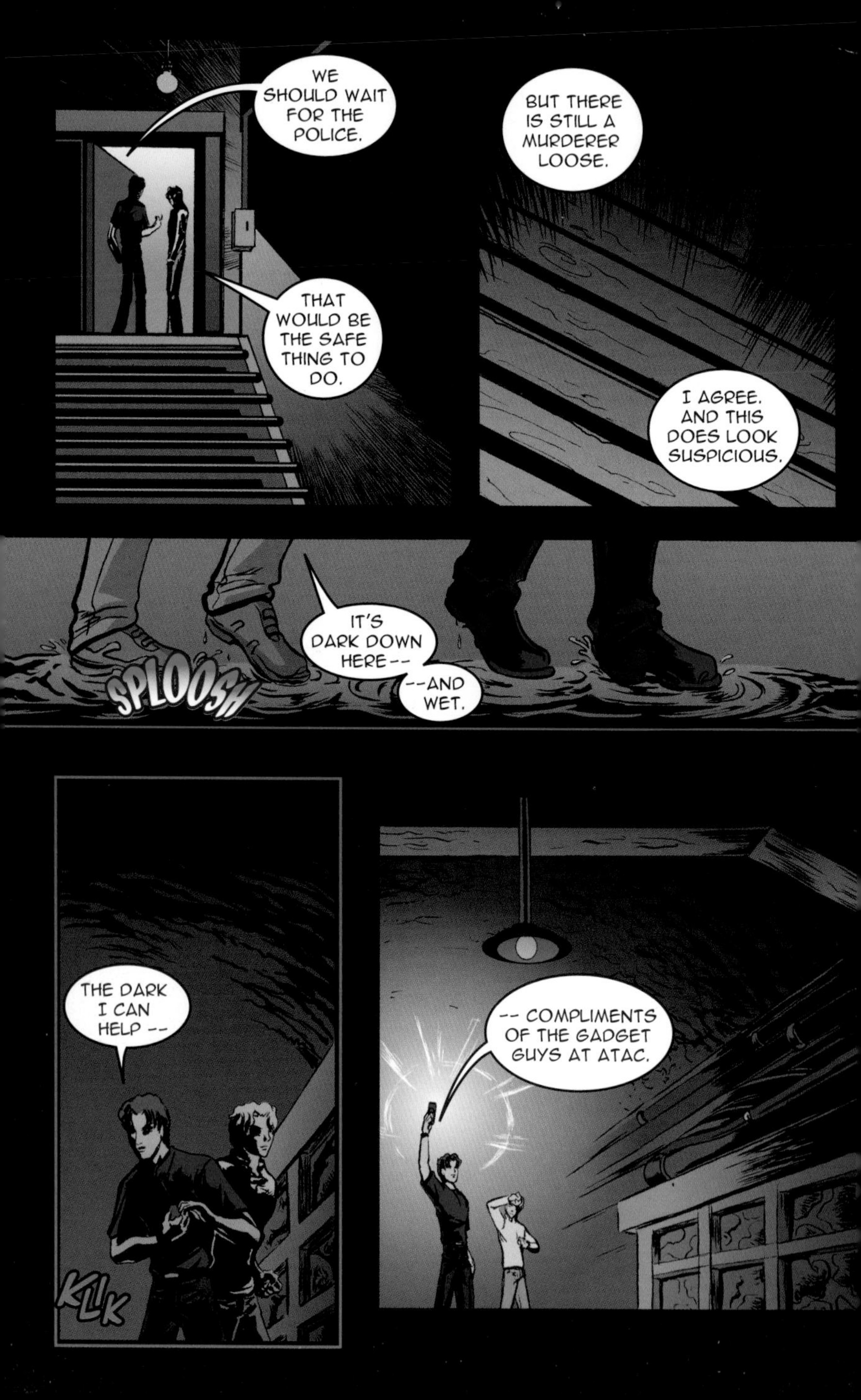
WE SHOULD WAIT FOR THE POLICE.
THAT WOULD BE THE SAFE THING TO DO.
BUT THERE IS STILL A MURDERER LOOSE.
I AGREE. AND THIS DOES LOOK SUSPICIOUS.
SPLOOSH
IT'S DARK DOWN HERE--
--AND WET.
THE DARK I CAN HELP --
KLIK
-- COMPLIMENTS OF THE GADGET GUYS AT ATAC.

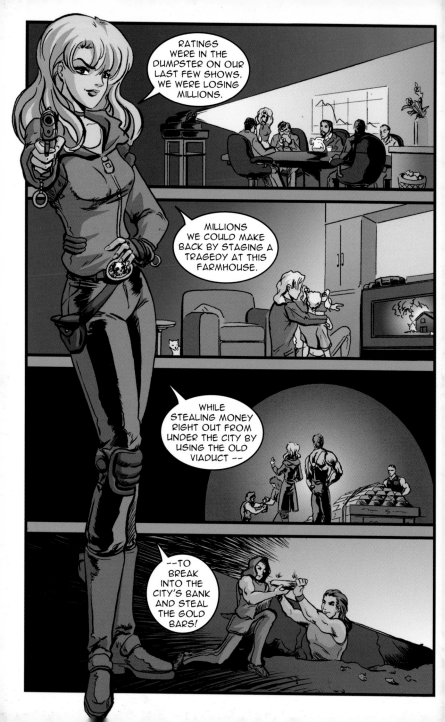

EPILOGUE:
"Home Again, Home Again..."

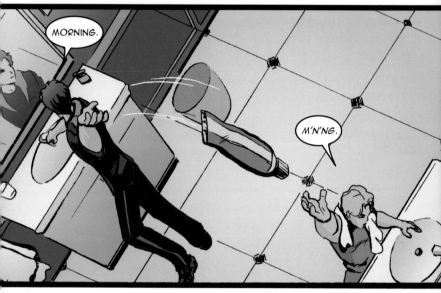

MORNING.

M'N'NG.

DO YOU MISS THOSE CAMERAS IN YOUR FACE EVERY MOMENT?

NOT ONE BIT, NO.

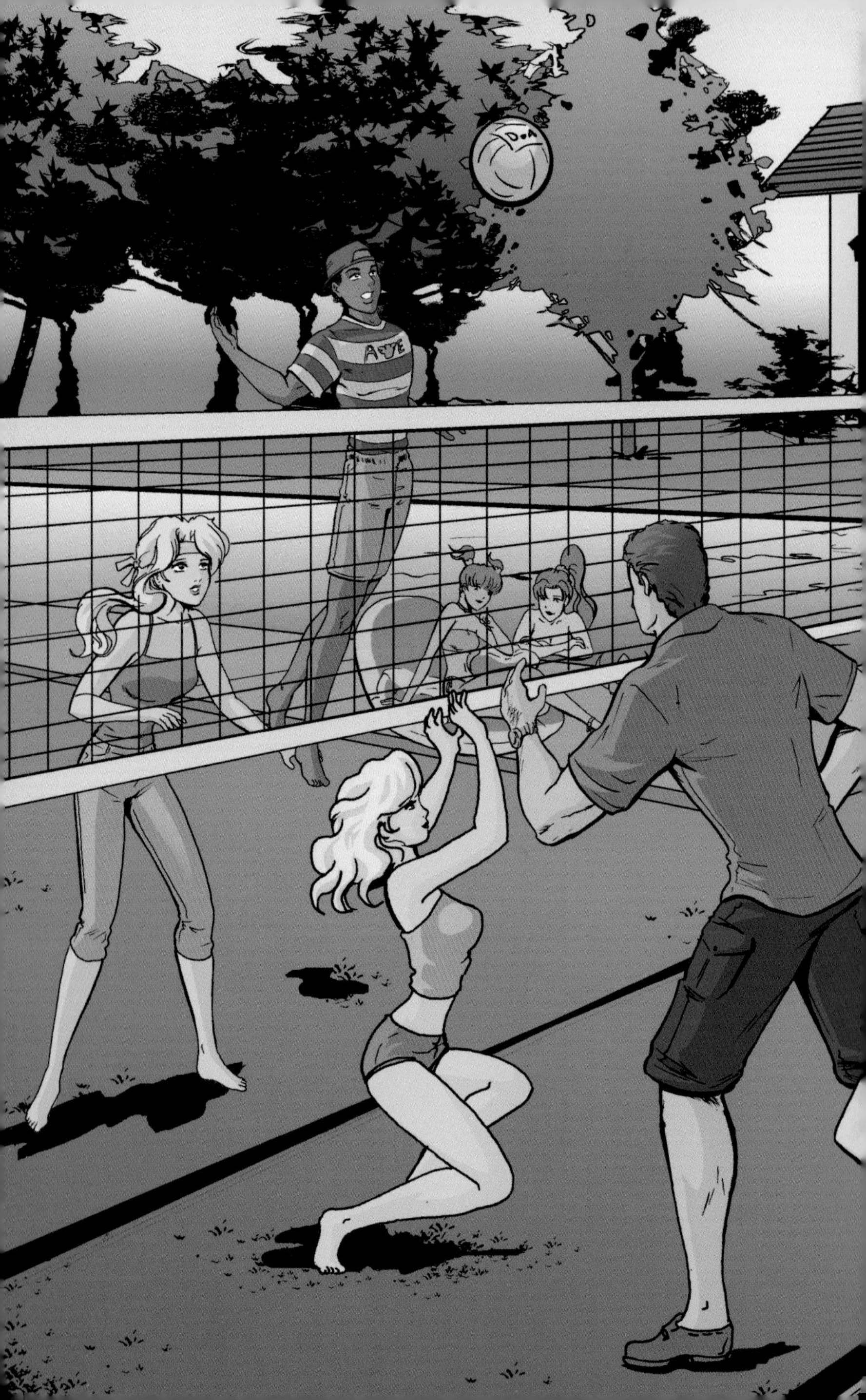

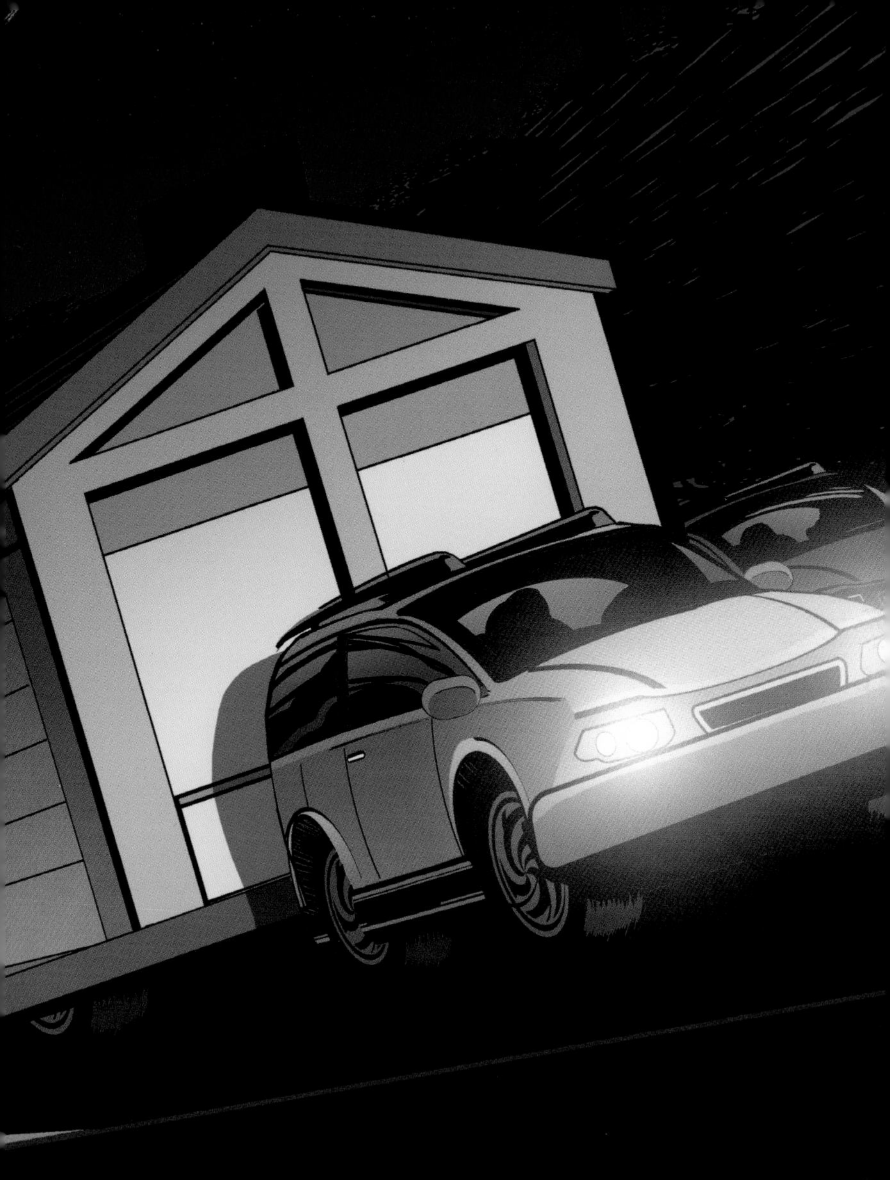

CHAPTER ONE:
"What A Long Strange Drive It's Been"

Don't miss THE HARDY BOYS Graphic Novel #4- "Malled"